DOUBLE SHOCK

He braced a shoulder hard against the door and shoved with all his strength. He heard the latch give and felt the door click open a scant quarter of an inch. He pushed his weight against it heavily and it gave way before his bulk.

He heard a woman's scream.

As he catapulted headfirst into the room, his eyes riveted on the bed. The two women on it struggled apart, wide-eyed in horror and shock.

One of them was Alison ...

MAN AMONG WOMEN

RANDY SALEM

CUTTING EDGE

ISBN-13: 978-1-952138-96-6

Published by
Cutting Edge Books
PO Box 8212
Calabasas, CA 91372
www.cuttingedgebooks.com

MAN AMONG WOMEN

CHAPTER ONE

E D WHELAN interrupted the bargaining session to nod toward the window.

"Now that kind of dame sends me!"

Ralph Thayer followed the man's gaze out the second-floor window to a redhead bobbing through Broadway traffic.

Ralph shrugged. "You're too predictable." He started gathering the photographs scattered across the desk and stacking them into a neat pile. "How about it, Ed? Three grand for these or no?"

"Will twenty-five hundred, and six pages from my little black book, do just as well?" Ed grinned.

"Sure," Ralph played the game, "if you can explain it to my girl."

"Chicken." Ed pinned down the photos with a finger. "Okay," he said, "take the three grand. But send me an underwater sequence to complete our next aquatic feature. You know—the usual. Lots of color and pretty fish. I'll need about fifteen shots for the spread."

Ralph sighed. "What a vacation."

"Anything wrong with it? You really got yourself some deal, boy. Charging off to the Bahamas with nobody to protect your chastity. I always have to take the wife and kids wherever I go." His voice lowered confidentially. "Just between us, Ralph, how many native girls' scalps do you rack up every year?"

Ralph slid the check up from under Ed's ballpoint. "Hundreds," he said, heading for the door. "Sometimes thousands."

"Tomahawk a couple for me, will you?" Ed called after him. "And don't forget my pictures."

Ralph shouldered his way through the mobs of summer tourists clustered in front of the Paramount waiting for the doors to open. At the curb he whistled. He gave the cabbie his address in Brooklyn Heights and settled back against the red plastic seat.

Would Ed Whelan howl if he knew the truth, Ralph told himself. Who would suspect that although he had never gotten around to marrying her, he had been faithful to Peggy all these years?

A half-hour of traffic, and the taxi stopped in front of a new buff-colored brick apartment house. A doorman in blue twill and gold braid came forward. Ralph paid, tipped and strode into the air-conditioned lobby, his gaze straight ahead, avoiding the ugly tile murals on the walls. The place was an abomination to him. He still fretted for the inconspicuous brownstone that Peggy had insisted he leave when publishers' checks had begun to roll in fat and frequent. That was right after he had proposed, and he knew she had intended this fancy apartment to be their home. As his secretary, she occupied one of the six rooms. As Peggy, his prospective wife, she ran the whole place and his life with it.

He knew it wasn't love that held him, but habit. He had stopped loving Peggy when he'd realized that she could never amount to more than a commonplace wife and mother, meticulous and monotonous. Her endless little concerns with dinner parties and what to wear and what so-and-so said about somebody else bored him infuriatingly. She was no longer a desirable woman for him to pursue. Rather, she was content, complacent, stifling. After marriage, she would be even more so.

But what, after all, was the use of looking elsewhere? Other women, he knew, were no different. Given love and a dependable income, the most fascinating spitfire went dowdy. He had seen this happen to the wives of his friends and to women he had once admired tremendously. A woman married to the man she loved was like yesterday's rice pudding. And he knew that Peggy would be just as stale. Maybe that was why he hadn't yet married her, why he couldn't marry her.

This was a reprehensible attitude, sure. But where was the woman who could share it—the woman who could give him no peace, who could match his restlessness with her own drive? He often wondered if such a creature actually existed anywhere. At those times he felt that if he didn't find her, warm and real, his whole life would turn to dust, the essence of himself dried and shriveled by sheer boredom with Peggy or meaningless affairs with other women.

He had expected Peggy to be puttering about the apartment, maybe packing his valise, waiting to kiss him goodbye. But the place was silent. He called her name. No answer. Walking into the kitchen, he saw a sheet of her green, scented stationery propped against the sugar bowl. He squinted to read the carefully precise lettering. She had gone to the hairdresser and would be back later. She sent him her love and, in the same sentence, admonished him not to forget to endorse Ed's check for deposit.

He grinned with unexpected relief, scribbled his name across the back of the check, then dashed off to his bedroom to pack. He wanted to be out and gone before she returned. He would leave her a note, saying things he knew he could never really mean.

Never mind the dullness of eleven and a half months of the year. There would always be these two weeks. ...

He glided with the blue damsel fish and spotted chub through water warm and peaceful to his skin. In the eerie green light spread stag horns, violet weeds, fragile webbings of coral. Carefully he swam among them, a string of pearl-like bubbles trailing from his air tank and rising giddily around him.

Though he moved at leisure, his direction followed a path threading the sharp razor corals and conducting him through the reef. He swam with the same sureness as the butterfly fish darting around laggard crabs and sea urchins, his limbs relaxed, moving rhythmically. From year to year he had returned to find new towers of coral blocking the way, or places where they had tumbled, leaving gaps for him to pass through. But always it took him no more than twenty minutes to swim from the outboard-powered boat into the lagoon and to the sandy beach on the island that was his.

Standing straight, blond hair darkened and dripping, he lifted the mask from his face and sloshed the remaining few yards to the shore. Only palms and terns had climbed this crest. Barren of human touch, it lay basking in the sun, calm, serene, just as he had remembered it. The island rose straight out of the sea like a bony finger pointing skyward. Except for the broad expanse of sandy beach on the leeward side, cut off from the open sea by a half-moon of submerged coral reef, the island was an uninhabitable pile of jagged rock.

Possibly a man could swim across the reef at high tide—Ralph had never tried to—but no boat could possibly get through and the beach had remained an isolated, untouched paradise to which he alone, he was sure, knew the underwater approach.

He sat down and pulled off tank, gloves and fins. Then he rolled over on his stomach and rested his chin on crossed arms, smelling the dryness and warmth of the sand with a sharp awareness. At last! This made all the rest of the year almost worthwhile.

He was about to close his eyes when bright color about thirty feet up the beach caught his attention. He blinked away the remaining droplets and slowly rose to his knees. Was he dreaming? Was it a mirage?

She lay prone and relaxed on a red blanket, a strip of white toweling covering her buttocks. Her naked back glowed warmly tan. Thick black hair, free of pins, tumbled about her shoulders. With slim arms and legs spread motionless, she seemed to be sound asleep. A bottle of suntan lotion glinted near one elbow. A red bathing cap lay on the sand.

My God, this just isn't possible, Ralph's thoughts raced. What was a girl like that—or any girl, for that matter—doing here? His glances probed the sand near her, then the strip of beach. No fins, no mask, no air tank. He knew it to be virtually impossible to anchor a boat within surface-swimming distance and, unless she were a creature of the sea, she could never have reached the island—his island!—without equipment. A sense of annoyance at this invasion of his privacy battled with a curiosity that had to be satisfied. Slowly he walked over to the blanket and stood in silent indecision as his eyes followed the curve of her spine until it dipped beneath the towel. Her limbs were finely tapered and delicately toasted to a warm, golden hue. Abruptly, almost involuntarily, he touched her calf with his toe.

Her leg recoiled instantly. She turned over. The towel fell way from her naked body. The civilized, well-trained, gentlemanly part of his nature knew that he should avert his eyes, but the male in him stared. He had never seen such nude perfection. Her body was gently sun-touched from head to foot, the skin velvety soft, the ample breasts firm and round. She made no effort to cover herself as she sat up. Her matter-of-factness reminded Ralph of the innocence of childhood before modesty and shame take root.

There was something quiet and vaguely distant about her, as though he had crashed in on far-off thoughts. Her smile was remote as she moved to one side of the blanket and nodded for him to take the other.

Though words flooded to his tongue, he could not get them out. He felt that he was wandering into a new dimension of existence, one filled with unchartered challenges and discoveries. He caught his breath, as an enormity of possibilities raced through his mind.

The blazing sun, the bleached white sand, the utter isolation and stillness played suggestively on his senses and, as he sat down, his eyes searched hers. In that instant, all questions and answers were totaled. As if in a state of deep hypnosis, he leaned over and kissed her. He found her mouth waiting for his. His hands moved upward into the thick hair that curled over his fingers. She did not push him away. He ran his fingers down her cheeks and cupped her face upward to his, studying the deep blue eyes, the delicate nose, the soft, feminine mouth. She returned his gaze with a steadfastness and certainty that penetrated the deepest recesses of his soul. He knew that he would never be free again, no matter how long he might live or where the paths of his life might take him.

Again he lowered his lips to hers and as he did so, he pushed her down on the blanket. She straightened her legs until her thighs were against his and then her body arched upward to him. He was no longer capable of thought. He became one of the elements, sea and wind, sand and sky, man and woman. He did not even need to explore her for he already knew her, had known her for eons. He bore down on her heavily and her legs wrapped around his as she made ready for him. The tips of her breasts were hard against his bare chest, her fingers dug into his back, her tongue explored his lips, his mouth. As his arms tightened about her fiercely, she surged against him with a spasm of desire that equalled his own.

Later he lay beside her, leaning on one elbow, gazing sometimes out to the gleaming water, sometimes into her serene eyes, and he was unconscious of the hours that slipped by until the half-hidden sun painted the horizon with long strokes of orange.

No words had been spoken. Only touch and look had served for the communication that needs no words, and Ralph dreaded the first sound that would break the spell. Had he dared, he would have simply returned to the mainland but, until he knew who she was and where she was from, he could not leave. He couldn't risk losing her—ever.

"We should be getting back," he said as gently as he could, taking one of her hands in his.

He thought he saw a fleeting expression of sadness cross her face. "Don't you like it here?" Her voice was full and rich and she spoke with the faintest trace of an accent, as though many languages had melted into her English.

"Yes, of course I like it here," he said. "It's getting late though. Won't people be expecting you?"

She shrugged indifferently and he suddenly felt her close herself away from him. "It doesn't matter," she said. "You go ahead."

"And leave you here alone?"

"I'm used to being alone. I like to be alone." She turned her head and avoided his eyes.

Baffled, he thought of the many questions he wanted to put to her. Why couldn't he just say, "Look, I'm Ralph Thayer from New York. Who are you? Where do you live?" Those were the questions he would have put to any other woman—normal, everyday questions—but she was not a normal, everyday woman and he felt that he would be trespassing.

"Today's was a strong sun," he ventured. "You'd better come back now."

"It doesn't bother me," she said. "I like the sun."

Silence fell between them and her expression told him that he was dismissed. "Maybe I'll see you later in town?" he asked hopefully.

She scooped up some sand and let the grains slowly drift through her fingers. "Perhaps," she said.

Frustrated and dismayed, he donned his equipment and headed straight for the water. He dove sharply without looking back. The coldness and the dull green light soothed the tension within his muscles and he moved deeper beneath the waves until he reached the first sea lawns of staghorn coral.

Its store bells tinkling in an idling southerly breeze, the fishing settlement of Kinderman lay in a rocky crescent above the bay. It was one of the busier places on the "mainland"—which in actuality was itself an island—and much frequented by tourists, who considered it "off the beaten track."

When he reached the village, Ralph paid the boat rental, scooped out his gear and started up the sharply pitched hill to his hotel. He had donned sneakers and an old army shirt which flapped over his trunks. He looked like any of the idlers who wandered in and out of the bars and the tackle shops or sat crookedly atop the rocks, except for the fact that his body bore only a light vacation tan while most of the others had been either born or burned black. Solidhipped women who helped with the nets and the other fishing paraphernalia plodded by, their bare feet flat and thick-soled, impervious to the pebbles that painfully jabbed Ralph's shoe-pampered skin. Sometimes a skinny urchin ran by, heading to or from one of the flat-roofed houses. No one seemed to pay any heed to anyone else.

The Hotel Kinderman boasted an iron bell in a turret and a fan in every room. It was the largest and only fairly habitable hotel in town. The wide entrance doors stood open so that those guests who preferred shade could sit in the lobby and look out and down into the shining bay. As Ralph entered, two people were sitting in the wicker chairs, each scanning a section of the previous Sunday's Tampa newspaper. One was Carlos Montrose, the desk clerk who could speak the language of anyone who came in to register. The other was the plump chambermaid who answered to the name of Clara. Only Montrose looked up.

"Two letters for you this morning." His voice had a paid-to-be-cheerful lilt that reminded Ralph of a young man on his first job after graduation. His smile was professionally pleasant. When he went behind the desk, the back of his linen suit showed a year-long gray and creased look about it.

Ralph took the letters and the key, nodded thanks to Montrose and walked up the carpeted stairs to his room. He dumped his swimming gear carelessly on the worn plush chair near the window and dropped onto the double bed. He reached with his foot to the switch on the wall and turned on the fan, then slipped the letters into his pocket. One, he knew, was from Peggy. The other was about his picture assignment. Neither interested him at the moment.

Piece by piece, Ralph went over the day in his mind. No matter how close to the island he had ever been able to anchor the boat before diving, it had always been impossible to reach the beach without an oxygen tank. And he happened to be an exceptionally good swimmer. Certainly that girl must have needed oxygen equipment, then, to get to the place. But if she had buried her gear to protect it from the sun, why so smoothly as to leave no sign? And how had she managed the blanket and the lotion?

He sat up abruptly and noticed that the clouds were tinged with pink. He had planned to develop some negatives and he was long overdue in writing to Peggy but suddenly, inexplicably, it became more important for him to get a haircut.

Kinderman boasted only one dining place where women who wore shoes would go. At ten minutes past seven, with the sun still glowing orange, Ralph went in and sat down at a corner table. The tablecloth lay white and smooth, decorated only with a green ashtray and a stub of candle low in a pottery jar. A menu was dropped in front of him.

"Whiskey sour." He handed back the menu.

"Waiting for a friend?" A barrel-like waiter in a soft bow tie smiled happily down at him. Few people dined here alone.

Ralph nodded. The business people of Kinderman knew him well and they welcomed him from year to year for he spent freely and made no demands on the native women. He knew some of them hoped that he might and that he would pay handsomely for the privilege, but he was not condemned for his abstention.

He sat in the corner, nursing his drink, and forced his mind to sort out the rest of the shots needed to complete the picture sequence for Ed. In ten days of shooting, the ocean had been neighborly enough to pose a giant blue starfish on a brain coral, some decorator crabs dressed in the camouflage of plants and an open-mouthed clam three feet long. But as yet he had seen neither barracuda nor sting ray, and Ed would need one or the other for the feature.

Ralph was tired of photographing pretty fish curving gracefully through calm waters. At first it had been exciting because the wide variety of form and color had been stimulating and thrilling to his senses, and the pictures he had taken back to Ed were stunning with scarlets and purples, blues and greens. But the true coral reef was no such fairyland and he was determined to give the predators their turn in the camera's eye.

He watched the sun slip down the sky until it seemed, suddenly, to drop past the horizon. The waiter set his third drink before him and lit the squat candle with a wooden match. His smile of pleasant expectancy for Ralph's evening had turned to forced words of encouragement and then to silence and a poker face, hiding the genuine sorrow in his heart. Ralph watched the gradual change and when, at a quarter of ten, it reached its final stage of dejection, he paid the bill and left. He could hardly refrain from telling the old fellow that things were not so sad as they seemed.

Until this time Ralph's mind had been occupied with his job and his thoughts had deliberately steered away from her, but as he went out into the night, the air throbbed with the scent of mountain flowers and the lighted town resembled a diamond ring lying curled beneath the sky's ebony blackness. People who had toiled hard during the day were giving themselves to dancing and open love-making. The sweet melody of guitars vibrated through the darkness. Where the hell was she?

With his jacket blowing open and his hands jammed into his pockets, he strode briskly downhill toward the rougher section of town. Later, he had to admit to being glad that he hadn't found her there.

By one o'clock most of Kinderman had exhausted itself. An occasional snore replaced the sound of guitars. The black huts seemed to settle back into the rocks and Ralph, his head aching from the tension of denied hope, turned around to walk back up the hill. There was only one other town on the island and it lay thirty miles up the coast. Had she gone there?

In his room he sat down near the open window to rest his throbbing legs. His whole body ached and his eyes were strained from the intensity of his search. In fact, he realized that he was still searching in the shadows as he gazed out the window. What did he expect—that she would float down from a star? Annoyed with himself and with her, he turned his back to the sky and his glance fell on the thin green envelope sticking out of his pocket.

As he pulled out the letter, he sighed tiredly, suddenly feeling old, foolish and frustrated, tied by his own choice to a fate tailor-made to his own weaknesses. After all, he had to admit there was really nothing wrong with Peggy. He had known what Peggy was the moment he had met her—but he had not known what he himself was. He had not foreseen that he would let her take over his life and have everything, including him, her own way. As he thought about it, he felt weak with shame.

The letter said nothing, of course. Her letters never did. It told him mostly that the weather was unbearably humid and would he please hurry home so they could go away together. He sighed. It was better than being alone, he supposed. At least he belonged some place. Someone depended on him, maybe even loved him. He folded the letter and promised himself that he would write to her in the morning.

The chaos of thoughts spinning in his head put sleep beyond him. Guilt about Peggy, his neglect and thoughtlessness of her, mixed with a hopelessly burning curiosity about the girl with the black hair and concern over how to find her. Finally he took out his Leica and a camel's-hair brush. He spent the rest of the night cleaning.

At sunrise, propelled by a current of excitement he could not control, he packed his diving gear and hurried out to fill his air tank. The fact that he had had neither food enough nor sleep enough to last him through the day lent a hazy kind of urgency to his mission. He ran all the way down the hill to the dock, kicking up pebbles and dust in his speed. He tossed his gear into the boat and pushed off from shore. Soon his island loomed before him. He anchored the boat, donned his apparatus, and went over the side.

Only the top layer of sand had been warmed by the new day's sun and Ralph emerged from the chilly water into the air still cool. In a moment his glance flashed around the oval of beach but found nothing to relieve the monotony of the smooth strand. The island once again looked as it always had, empty and lonely. He buried his gear beneath the sand and sat down with his back against a rock, watching the sea and listening for the sound of a human being breaking the surface of the water. For hours he sat motionless, but there was nothing to disturb the glimmering sea and the whisper of ripples slapping gently upon the shore.

Slowly the tide rose. Ralph watched it inching across the beach, thinking ruefully that this was exactly what he had done for five summers with utter contentment.

The sun had climbed halfway up the sky before he saw the red bathing cap in the distance. Shading his eyes with his hand and squinting, he watched for a few minutes as her arms propelled her easily through the water. When he was certain that she was moving toward shore, he lay back in relief and closed his eyes.

After what seemed like hours and countless pangs of fear that she had changed her mind and decided to turn back, he heard the splash of water dragging at her ankles and then he heard her walking up the beach toward him. Hardly daring to breathe, he tried to lie still, his eyes shut tight, his heart thumping violently.

Suddenly the sun was blocked from his face. He opened his eyes and looked up into hers.

She pulled off her cap and shook out her hair. He watched the easy, graceful movement of her body as she bent to one side and fluffed out the damp strands with the forked fingers of one hand. Drops of water hung from her dark eyelashes and ran down her neck, her bathing suit, her thighs. Yesterday he had thought her very young. She still seemed young to him but not so much through lack of years as through lack of burdens. She was the most relaxed creature he had ever seen. While her eyes were wide in greeting, there was a peculiar, expressionless quality to them. It was as though she were instinctively shielding herself against intrusion.

"So you like it here, too," she said. She did not look at him but tilted her face to the sun and blinked the water from her eyes. For a moment her hands caressed her hips. Then she unhooked what he had thought was the belt of her suit and from it rolled a short spread which she placed on the sand beside him.

He recalled the previous day's insane joy and searched for the words to recapture the mood. "It's not just the place," he said. He thought his voice sounded stilted and foolish but she did not seem to notice his nervousness.

She sat down. "You're sweet."

"Will you come back into the water for a while?"

"Not yet. I want to rest."

"All right," he said, "but while you're resting, how about telling me how you get here?" Since there was not enough room on the spread, he sat beside it on the sand, sifting the fine grains through his fingers.

"Same way you get here."

"I have fins and a mask and a tank. The works. Where are yours?"

"I'm not a beginner," she said simply.

"Beginner, hell," he said harshly. "Have you been swimming under water for thirty years?"

She smoothed the spread. "I didn't mean swimming." Again her voice had a distant quality.

He stopped sifting the sand and turned to look at her, trying to pin down the elusive quality in her manner. His sensation of intruding on her was constantly contradicted by the rest of her carefree ways.

"What did you mean, then?" he asked.

"Oh, just things," she said. "All kinds of things." Her face was expressionless.

"I don't understand."

"Yes, you do."

"No. Truly."

She shrugged her shoulders, turned her back to him and stretched out full length in the sun, closing her eyes. "Well, maybe some day you will."

"But you do get here without an air tank, don't you?" he persisted.

"I didn't say that."

"Well, I'd like you to explain."

"Later, maybe. Now let's talk about something else."

"All right. Last evening. I looked for you three hours. Where the hell were you?"

"Hell yourself," she said, showing a hint of annoyance. "If this is going to turn into a question and answer session, we might just as well go in swimming." She sat up and began pushing her hair back into the red cap.

Ralph hardly had time to feel chastised. He snatched his fins and mask, jumped up and ran after her as she shallow-dived into the warm water. Without the aid of equipment she swept ahead of him so easily that he soon felt like a lobster behind a seal. With amazement he followed her as she knifed along, the lithe body propelled by legs as able as those of any creature born to the sea.

He gave up trying to overtake her and struggled only to keep her in sight. She was not trying to lose him for she turned occasionally to see if he were still behind her and he could see her smile. Far less often than he had thought possible for any human being, she moved to the surface to gulp air and then streaked down again. Returning to him, she sat on his back for a few moments and rode him like a jockey, but when he turned over and tried to put his hands about her waist, she slipped free and surfaced again.

Parrot fish and needle-like urchin fish watched them from safe distances. Gradually Ralph put aside the years of training and practice which had taught him to go slowly in order to preserve his wind. He moved after the swift, darting image and, when it playfully hesitated, caught up with it. He touched her skin and found it cool and smooth. They tumbled and lazed seal-like on the silt bottom, legs touching legs, palms gliding over backs, the front of her bathing suit moving across the bare skin of his chest. He would rather have drowned than return to the air, sun and sand above.

Yet it was that need for air that forced him, finally, to the surface. He stood in the shallow water and waited for her, and in a few minutes she followed him ashore.

They fell down together at the edge of the beach, ignoring the spray of water lapping over their feet. He unhooked her cap and pulled it off. Her hair tumbled down, rich and luxuriant.

"Are you always in such a hurry?" she asked, pulling away from him a little. "I like to be slower about things."

"Okay," he said. "Slower it will be." And as gently as he could, he slid the straps off her shoulders and pushed them down until her breasts were revealed, damp and pearly smooth. Carefully he toweled her dry, raising first one slim arm and then the other. She was relaxed and complacent, regarding him with laughter shining in her eyes as he meticulously dried her from head to foot.

Then he bent over her and slowly the shadows of their curved bodies blended into one on the sand. Beads of sea water dried and were replaced by those of passion. As before, there were no words between them. None were needed. He knew how to love her skillfully, draining her and himself of every drop of desire, of need, of strength. She sighed in deep contentment and closed her eyes.

"Slow enough?" he asked.

She nodded. "You're learning," she said. "Better than most."

"Most?"

"Most men," she answered, her eyes still closed.

It almost sounded like an insult but he was not sure of her meaning. Besides, he was too spent, too contented to argue and he, too, closed his eyes. In sleep his arm moved around her shoulder and pulled her close.

They awoke together to the lapping of the tide against their thighs. He pulled her with him up to the dry sand. He felt the need for food and covering against the oncoming evening coolness. He thought for a moment of Kinderman waiting like a jaded tart to welcome him. He thought of the hotel with its warped floors, its rusty fans and its dirt.

He thought of the previous night and the waiter and the sweet melody of the guitars.

He turned to face her. "How would you like to brave it here with me until morning?"

She looked at him, a smile starting in her eyes. "Now you're getting the idea."

CHAPTER TWO

THE BIG problem, of course, was food. Nothing edible grew on the coral island. But diligent search up and down the beach, and among the sunken shelves of coral off shore, yielded not exactly a harvest but at least a fair selection of sea creatures—a couple of crabs, a few clams, several mussel-like bivalves, and a double handful of what might have been large shrimp but more likely were prawns. All these, perforce, were devoured raw.

With their hunger satisfied and the warm sand as a blanket for two, Ralph knew there was nothing in all of civilization that he wanted. The girl beside him rested her head on his shoulder and, like himself, seemed to have all in life that she could ever desire. Gradually the sun dropped into the sea and together they watched the long strokes of gold and purple paint the horizon. A pale star glimmered. The moon rose and bathed in silver the two figures close on a grain of land.

The night seemed to pass in a fragile moment. Ralph awoke to find himself breathless with anticipation of dreams about to come true. He wiggled carefully out from the sand, trying not to disturb her, but a pile of the grains slipped from the girl's body and she awoke, shivering in the sunrise chill. He tried to cover her again.

"It's no use," she said, sitting up and brushing the sand from her neck and arms. "Oh, what a cold morning. Hand me the spread, will you?"

They had used it for a pillow. He picked it up and shook it out away from her, then handed it to her. "That won't be warm enough."

She shrugged. "It'll do until the sun gets stronger." She took it from him and wrapped it around herself like a stole.

"If I could just get out to the boat and bring back my shirt—" he began.

"Why bother?" she asked, shading her eyes and looking off to the horizon. "It'll warm up pretty soon. And the fewer things we have that will get sandy, the better."

"Then fine, if you don't mind eating sea food again for breakfast."

"Have I a choice?"

"Look," he said, trying not to sound impatient, "the point is, if I could get to the boat, I could bring some things back from the mainland. Then we'd really be set." He had no intention of letting her get away from him again.

"What things, for instance?"

"Well, clothing. And some dry wood so we don't have to eat everything raw." He raised his hands in a restless gesture. "Maybe a bottle of wine to go with dinner."

"And toothpaste?"

"If you wish."

"How about an umbrella to shade off the sun and a couple of books to read when we get tired of swimming?" she asked in an utterly serious tone.

Something about it made him look at her uneasily. "Making fun of me, hey?"

"Oh, I'm not. Not really. It just gets so tiresome, the way people are always wanting to change things. And always thinking they're changing them for the better. My father, for example," she said unexpectedly. "That poor man devoted the last fifteen years of his life to changing me from a snotty brat to a mascara-ed debutante. Then he died and left me free to change myself right back again. If he had left me alone and looked after himself—"

"You'll probably do the same for your own kids some day," he said.

"Maybe you will, but I'll see myself dead before I'll let my own children make a fool of me," she said with feeling. "Anyway, if you don't like things the way they are here, please just get to your boat and go."

Even her back, which she turned to him abruptly, was perfect. Life in abundance, his only chance for true happiness, centered in her. What more could he want?

He turned her around to face him. "My name is Ralph Thayer," he said pleasantly. "Would you prefer sun-broiled lobster or a crab cocktail?"

From that moment on, the island was changed from a secluded hide-out under the stars to an open-air palace filled with rare luxuries and sensuous delights. Time drifted into hours, the hours into days. Their food supply was limited chiefly to the slow-moving shelled creatures of the deep, to clams, shrimp and crabs, but it proved quite able to sustain life.

His tan deepened to a healthy bronze and his thoughts became less anxious. He began to feel himself one with nature's great cycle of growth, change, destruction and rebirth. What did it matter if they thought he had stolen a boat? There was enough money in the bureau drawer back at the hotel to pay for it. His cameras? Lenses? He hoped that whoever took them would remember to take the cleaning chamois too.

Nothing mattered except that this girl stay with him—or rather, that she let him stay with her.

In the days that followed he learned that her name was Alison and that no one ever called her by a shorter form of it. The days and nights seemed somehow to blend into one another so that time ceased to move. He found himself telling her how he had found the island by accident the first time he had come to the reef on a photo assignment. And he told her a little bit about Peggy.

Not urged for the details of his life, he nevertheless poured out his resentment toward Peggy and the demands of his work. Alison never interrupted him nor did she appear particularly interested. She would play with a clam shell or clean a few grains of sand from beneath a fingernail. Sometimes she even dozed. He knew she cared little, if at all, about his past life; and of his future, what was there to say? The moment was now, eternal, for she must realize as well as he that, with his diving tank nearly empty, he was—whether he wanted to be or not—stranded on the island. He did not have enough air left to reach his boat and the mainland. Occasionally he would think about it and resent his helplessness. He sensed that she could leave him any time she wanted to and he was almost afraid to sleep at night lest he might awaken some morning and find himself alone.

Studying her for the smallest indications of her mood put a strain on him although she seemed contented enough. She lolled through the days, swimming or relaxing on the beach, and she continued to crave him like a newlywed. There was hardly a grain of sand on the island that had not known the weight of their bodies—whether on the dry beach, at the ocean's edge or half slipping into the water. Only the sea itself had eluded them.

One morning while they sat watching a snail tediously push itself back into the water after it had been washed ashore, he said simply, "You have never told me how you came here."

She reached out to push the snail with her toe. "Don't worry about that," she said. "You'll know soon enough. All this won't last forever."

He looked at her closely. Her features remained placid but her voice held an edge of regret. His heart contracted in a spasm of fear.

"Don't tell me," he said quickly. "It's not that important."

"You want to know. You will have to know."

He stood up. "Please forget that I mentioned it." He turned and dashed into the water.

But he had created a rift by his curiosity.

When he emerged from the water, she let him make love to her and, for the first time, he felt that she was not really with him. Fear flooded icily through his veins and suddenly he nearly panicked. He knew that he could never return to Peggy after this, to dinner parties and proper ties and more of the same dull years. His one chance to save himself, to make the rest of his life worthwhile, lay with this girl. He dare not lose her. Whatever she might do, wherever she might go, he must stay with her.

Ralph forced himself into a semblance of nonchalance. He did not comment on her cold kisses and when her once eager body no longer surged upward to meet his own, he said nothing. But at night while she slept beside him, he stared gloomily out at the dark waves, feeling as cold and as miserable as though he were already alone.

Alison took to making sand sculptures down by the water's edge and she would dawdle over them for hours like a child. From a distance he watched her, knowing that she no longer thought of him. Uneasily he realized that she was just marking time, that she was waiting for something or someone. If she had ever cared for him at all, why hadn't she at least given him some warning of this change instead of suddenly withdrawing from him? Her elusiveness carried a peculiar quality that made her seem essentially inviolate, taboo, and filled him with foreboding.

One morning as the sun reached toward the center of the cloudless sky, Ralph noticed a dark speck on the horizon out beyond the reef. It looked suspiciously like a shark's fin and he hastily called it to Alison's attention.

To his surprise, she jumped up eagerly from the blanket and squinted seaward in the direction of his pointing finger. Questioningly he turned to her and saw a smile widen the lovely lips into a gleeful grin. He half expected to see her clap her hands and jump up and down with joy. Instead, she rubbed her thigh in silent delight as she strained forward to see more clearly.

"It's about time," she whispered. "About time." She was completely unaware of him.

Puzzled, he said nothing but divided his glance between her and the black speck that was slowly becoming larger as it neared the shore.

"It'll be quite a while yet," she said. "I might just as well sit down." She kneeled to tug a crease out of the blanket and then lowered herself to it, leaning back on the palms of her hands. For some time she sat quietly gazing out over the water, the smile still on her face.

Ralph saw the life return to her eyes. They held the same expression that they had when she had first seen him. The look had been gone for so long that now it made him uncomfortable. He was too nervous to sit still. He stood, straining his eyes to see what caused her such joy. It seemed to move with painful slowness. Fifteen, twenty minutes passed and still he could not make out what it was. Certainly it was no sailing craft. It was much too small. Watching the straight course it took toward them, he wondered if it would be coming in through the reef. The tide was high and it could possibly get across the jagged points of coral. Alison offered no explanation. Indeed, she seemed to have forgotten his presence entirely. He wanted to shout at her, to shake her, but a choking fear stopped him.

When he could endure the suspense no longer, he stepped into her line of vision. "What in hell's out there anyway?" he demanded angrily.

She looked up at him but he knew that her eyes did not see him. "Relax, darling. Have some crab meat," she said absent-mindedly.

"I'm not hungry."

"Then lie down and take a snooze."

"How can I sleep at a time like this?"

"Oh, come on now," she said soothingly. "Sit down. You shouldn't upset yourself like this."

Suddenly he realized that she was mocking him. He felt breathless with a screaming fury. She lifted her hand to his in what he thought was a gesture of reassurance and he let her pull him down beside her. He waited for her to speak, to tell him what was going on, but her attention returned at once to the sea. Defeated and miserable, he rolled over on his stomach and pressed his eyes against his arm.

He felt the girl move beside him and then heard her brush the sand from her legs. Her new, lively manner not only told him quite plainly that she was eager to be away from him but also that he was not to try to follow her.

Still, he knew that he would pursue her, that he would cling to her so tenaciously that, in the end, she would have to give in to him. Nothing else would ever do. And because she had wanted him in utter surrender once, she would want him again, he knew. And he knew too that some day he would have to understand and come to grips with whatever strange force it was that pulled her from him now.

"You can look if you want to," she said blandly. Her voice cut sharply across his thoughts.

Ralph sat up and turned to stare at what had been a mere dot on the water. He saw a bobbing, shaggy head held high above paddling feet.

"A dog?" he exclaimed incredulously.

She stood up and shook the last grains of sand from her blanket. "Pretty, isn't he? His name is Mars."

"But how did he know to come here?"

"He's half homing pigeon." She found her discarded bathing suit nearly buried in the sand and stepped into it, pulling it up slowly over her brown hips. His heart filled with despair, Ralph watched her fit her ample breasts into the cups of the suit.

"But how does he know when to come?"

She did not answer him. The waves had brought Mars close to shore and he was wading the rest of the way. Alison ran down to meet him, unmindful of the shower he shook off his thick, black hair. Tied around the animal's body was a thin nylon cord with which Alison pulled in a large aluminum box lashed to a ship's life preserver. Mars stood still obediently while she untied the rope, then he ran up the beach and rolled luxuriously in the sand.

Ralph watched her remove from the box a set of fins and air tanks, a mask, heavy cotton gloves and two cans of dog food. He was considerably relieved. He had half expected a helicopter to come in and swoop her away, but this was back in his league.

She opened the containers of dog food with a can-opener thoughtfully taped to one of them, and took them up the beach to the animal. Ralph watched them as they sat together, the dog hulking enormous beside her slimness, but gentle as he ate from her fingertips. It occurred to Ralph that Mars was probably kinder in many ways than was his mistress.

She lingered with the animal, stroking his thick neck and putting her cheek to his nose while she spoke to him in a low, crooning voice. Waiting to see what would happen next, Ralph dug up his own equipment and began to check it. He frowned over the air tank, praying to himself that he had enough gulps of air to get him through the reef. For all he knew, the lines might be clogged with sand. It was just one of the risks he had to take. His life seemed all risks now anyway.

After Mars had rested, Alison led him back to the water. As he started to swim out, she hastily slipped on the fins and adjusted the breathing apparatus on her shoulders. Ralph, taking his cue from her, climbed into his own gear.

"You coming along?" She tugged at the tank straps to adjust them along her thighs.

"Just for the ride," he said as noncommittally as he could.

"Well, that's your business, of course. But you'd better be prepared for a few changes."

He glanced briefly at her bathing suit and smiled. "I've already had some."

She shrugged and moved out into the waves.

Grimly, Ralph followed.

CHAPTER THREE

FOLLOWING Alison back to the mainland turned out to be the easiest part of Ralph's plan. She swam leisurely through the corals, carefully avoiding the narrow passages in favor of wider and safer routes.

They surfaced in view of a large cabin cruiser with the name *Jim Boy* newly painted on the white hull. Ralph pushed back his mask and spat out the rubber-tasting mouthpiece. They made it just in time for he had been gasping for air. He treaded water beside her, waiting for her to make the next move. As he watched the rope ladder drop over the side and splash into the sea, he wondered if she would invite him aboard.

She said nothing to him and he clambered up the slippery rungs behind her. On deck, a giant black man waited. His ebony muscles gleamed and rippled as he served them towels and drinks and then made off toward the bow with their swimming gear. Without waiting for an invitation, Ralph sat down on one of the three blue canvas chairs and stared for the first time at the blackness of his sunburned skin.

"I feel like a native version of Rip van Winkle," he said, trying to make conversation with her. He touched his chin, feeling the wiry growth with his fingertips. The varnished deck beneath his feet, the gentle roughness of the cloth against his back and the coldness of the glass in his hand brought back the familiar world he had nearly forgotten. Life with her on the island—the silent days and the restless nights—suddenly fell into place as memory.

He looked closely at her, standing lithe and brown at the railing, and saw a rich, spoiled and bored girl.

Less than half an hour later, Mars reached the side of the boat and was taken on board to sprawl exhausted on the deck. Then the huge Negro started the motor and they moved off in the direction of Ralph's hired boat. Alison had been good enough to consent to pick it up and tow it to the mainland.

An hour or so afterward Ralph stepped to the dock and into the bustle of life ashore. Idle fishing boats lay bobbing from anchored buoys. Fishermen and their women fussed over the salty nets spread to dry on the sand. He watched a man strike a match with his fingernail and lift the flaring light to a cigarette. The remembered taste of tobacco filled him with a sudden craving and he reached automatically to his pants pocket, but he knew he had neither cigarettes nor the money with which to buy them. He had nothing to his name but a pair of trunks and the memory of days spent on an island with a girl named Alison.

He turned to look for her. She was walking briskly up the landing, her body swinging jauntily inside a white sharkskin skirt and a sheer rose-colored blouse that scarcely concealed her ample breasts. He watched her with a pang of regret for, fully clothed, she seemed farther away from him than ever before. She wore white, spike-heeled shoes and they clicked a calypso against the warped boards of the landing. A few paces behind her stalked the giant attendant, his black eyes peering intently past her. When his wide lips spread into a grin, Ralph turned to follow his line of vision.

Beneath a wide silk parasol gripped firmly in a gloved hand, the woman sat quietly watching Alison approach. The woman's escort perched on the wooden seat of a donkey cart, the reins slack in his hands. Ralph instantly recognized the graying linen suit although he had never before seen Montrose outside of the hotel. The man's head hung slightly, like the donkey's, causing him to appear small and shrunken beside the woman's dignified erectness.

She did not once remove her eyes from the girl's face, neither did she lean forward to greet her. Her expression remained inscrutable. Alison went directly to her and quietly, intimately, they exchanged a few words of greeting. Ralph noticed a striking resemblance in their profiles. Even their thick black hair was similar except that the woman's was shorter and streaked with silver, adding an air of authority and distinction to her handsome features. And when she motioned imperiously with her chin, Alison climbed into the wagon like an obedient child. The vehicle rattled away up the hill toward the hotel, leaving Ralph behind.

He watched until they were out of sight, wondering why the hell Alison let herself be dictated to that way. She had even left her dog behind. Ralph stalked up the hill after the cart, too angry and all of a sudden too worried to feel the rocky ground beneath his bare feet.

When he reached the hotel, Montrose was already busy behind the desk checking through entries in an old, smeary ledger. As Ralph approached, Montrose looked up and nodded blandly.

"The *Señor* has returned?" He smiled ingratiatingly. He seemed unaware of Ralph's irritation.

"Yes. Now, let's have the key."

"Key?" Montrose said mildly.

"The key to my room, dammit. Now come on. I haven't got all day." Ralph tapped the top of the counter with the base of his fist.

Montrose shook his balding head. "I am sorry, *Señor*," he said politely. "You used up the time you paid for. Now I will have to rent the room to you all over again."

Ralph gestured impatiently. "That's all right with me. But where's all my stuff?"

Montrose bent down and from under the counter brought out the cameras in their neat leather cases. Carefully he lined them up side by side. "You will find this is everything," he said.

Ralph's glance quickly took in the array. "How about my clothes?"

Montrose dragged out the familiar blue suitcase and pushed it across the counter. Ralph turned the bag on its side and unsnapped the latches. His clothes lay neatly folded, the suit on its hanger inside the top lid.

"Okay," he said. "Now sign me up again."

"You wish to pay in advance?" Montrose dipped the pen into a bottle of ink and wiped the tip.

"Sure, sure." He pulled the pants off the metal hanger of the valise and put his hand quickly into each pocket. He swore under his breath. The wad of bills was gone.

Montrose was watching him as he searched and when he finally looked up, the clerk shook his head. "Something is missing?"

Ralph sighed. "No."

"How long do you wish to stay?"

"I'm not sure. Maybe another week. Maybe longer." He lifted the Hasselblad off the counter and held it out to Montrose. "You take this instead of money?"

Montrose hesitated as though the idea were unexpected. Then he smiled, showing the tips of yellowed, overlapping teeth. "For you, I take it," he said. He put the camera back beneath the counter.

Once again Ralph lugged his belongings across the lobby and up the stairs. He stopped at the first landing and stood still, listening for sounds of voices or movement in the rooms that lined the long hall. The women must be there somewhere, he felt sure, but the floor was quiet. He dragged his gear into his room and let it lie just inside the door. Then he caught sight of his reflection in the mirror on the opposite wall. He stared at it curiously. The blond hair and eyebrows were bleached almost white and they stood out starkly against his tanned face. His frame had slimmed down and his muscles were as hard as they had been in his early youth. He looked as savage as he felt, his browned loins barely covered by the skimpy cloth of his bathing trunks.

But the image of himself did not hold his interest for long. His attention was caught by the sound of solid, rather heavy footsteps in the room directly above. He listened intently for the sound of lighter, more delicate steps, but in vain. He sat down on the chair by the window and waited, his ears straining. He heard only the single pair of footsteps and soon they too were silent.

He hurried out of his room and up to the second landing. His attention concentrated on the door directly above his but he heard nothing. He felt like pounding on it with his fists and demanding to know where Alison was, but he realized that he would have to be far more tactful and play his hand with a calculated strategy—at least until he knew exactly how things stood.

Hastily he went back to his own room, took a quick shower and shaved, all the while keeping his ears cocked for the slightest sound from the room above. He dressed as properly as his wardrobe allowed and combed the tangles from his long hair.

Then again he went up to the second floor and straight down the hall to the room. He rapped loudly on the door. He had meant that the knock be light but his jumpy nerves defeated his control.

There were no sounds of movement from behind the door. He waited a few minutes, then rapped again. At last he heard footsteps and in a moment the door was opened a few inches. He saw Alison. She wore a transparent negligee which she was holding together at the throat with one hand.

Ralph felt his face flush and he swallowed hard. "Perhaps ... er ... may I take you and your companion to dinner this evening?" he stammered, trying to keep his voice even and steady.

She shook her head slowly and her eyes closed for a fraction of a second. "Not this evening, thank you," she said. "I'm awfully tired." Before he could say anything more, she shut the door in his face.

He stepped back in annoyance, listening for the sound of her bare feet padding across the wooden floor, but there was only silence. For some reason, he was furious. The footsteps he had first heard were not Alison's. He could have sworn to it. She could never possibly walk that heavily. Why the hell were they both so silent in there anyway? What was going on? Suddenly his scowl darkened. It couldn't be that ... A sudden chill whipped through him and he shivered.

For what seemed hours he stood there listening, keyed to the pitch of obsession. Something would happen. It had to. Some noise, some sound of movement or voice would reach his ears and give him an inkling of what was happening behind that door. All he had to do was stand there long enough. He had to know something. Anything.

His thoughts churned.

Both of them were in that room. Of that he felt certain. All right, so they weren't moving around, they weren't talking. Yet if they were simply resting, why together? Why not each in her own room? Uneasily he leaned back against the opposite wall, the questions multiplying in his mind.

The minutes dragged by until, reluctantly, he turned away and went back downstairs to continue his vigil. He knew that Alison could not go down the steps without his hearing her. He sat—it seemed an eternity—without cigarettes or food, afraid to leave the room, his door ajar in readiness. Night came on, bringing cool, clear air and cold, bright stars, and still he remained motionless in the dark.

And finally he heard the soft padding of a girl's feet not descending the stairs, but climbing them. He rose quickly, went to the door and saw Clara, her heavy body ascending slowly to the landing. He called a greeting to her and she paused, smiling at him under the dim hallway bulb. The skin around her slanted eyes crinkled into laugh lines and she was honestly glad to see him.

"You came just in time to take my dinner order," he said cheerfully.

"*Si*. But first I go up and take the ladies their soap and towels from the closet." She rolled her eyes skyward. "They say I forgot them, but I didn't."

"Two ladies staying upstairs?"

She nodded. "And cranky ones, *verdad*. I know I didn't forget their soap."

"Well, if two guests call down from two different rooms," Ralph said, "it looks like maybe you—"

Clara flicked her wrists impatiently through the air. "No, they both are in the one room."

Ralph smiled to himself, absently watching her as she lumbered up the second flight of steps. Missed my calling, he thought. Should have been a sleuth.

Dinner was a new problem to worry about. What the devil was he going to use for money? He knew he couldn't live for a week on the little that his cameras would bring. Montrose might advance him some, but it was that lousy thief's fault that he was in this fix in the first place. He needed money and lots of it. He didn't know when he might have to suddenly take off after Alison or where she might lead him. Quite simply, he would have to cable collect to the States for money. Ed would advance him a grand for the pictures. He'd be mad as hell, though. The damn things were more than a week overdue now. Suppose Ed sent only a hundred just to push him into action. Well, he'd have to take that chance. The cable would have to sound real urgent. He'd always played it square with Ed. Ed would trust him.

He hurried down the stairs and into the lobby. If he made the call from his room, he knew that Montrose would listen in.

However, if he called from the lobby, he might have some privacy. But, no, when Montrose saw him head for the phone, he slid away from the desk and sat in one of the old, sagging wing chairs. He picked up a magazine. It was the same magazine the man always read, Ralph noticed, and he turned his back in frustration, knowing that Montrose would listen to every word he said.

When the message had been placed, Ralph crossed the lobby and sat down opposite Montrose. He glared at him. He wanted to pick up the little insect and smear him against the wall. Calmly the man put aside the battered magazine, sat back and crossed his legs. He smiled benignly.

"The house will not charge you for that call," he said.

Ralph stood up and swallowed his anger. "Thanks," he muttered, jamming his hands into his pockets and turning away to pace the worn rugs. There was no place he could go until he got the money, nothing he could do but wait. It had just better arrive before Alison decided to take off.

Ralph suddenly thought of Peggy and remembered with a pang of conscience that he had been due back home long ago. He had forgotten to send her a note, indeed he had almost forgotten her altogether. She would be frantic.

He called to Montrose, "Have there been any letters for me?"

Montrose went around behind the desk and found a week-old cable from Ed demanding the pictures, but there was nothing else. Peggy must be holding off until she heard from him. Ralph knew that he should put in a longdistance call to her but the idea was repugnant. He would have to lie and she wouldn't believe him anyway. He decided to cable her, saying that he had been delayed by damaged equipment.

While he was phoning, Clara came into the lobby and he motioned for her to wait. Breathing heavily, she dropped into an overstuffed chair and pulled a flowered handkerchief from the puff of her sleeve. She was still mopping her face when Ralph, the cable sent, hung up the receiver and crossed the lobby. He stood over her and spoke quietly.

"Can you bring three dinners or shall I call the restaurant and have them sent over with the boy?"

She gave a long sigh and spread her legs, fanning air between her thighs with the material of her full skirt. "No, *Señor. Estoy ransado yo*—too tired. You best send for the boy."

Suddenly he was in a quandary. If he ordered dinner directly from the restaurant, he would have to pay cash for it. If he got it through the maid, she would have it put on his hotel bill. He hadn't thought that she would say no—it meant that she would lose a nice tip. Perhaps if he waited a while, she would rest and cool off.

As he stood there indecisively, Montrose silently walked behind Clara and, bending over, leaned an arm on her chair.

"She will get you the dinners, *Señor*," he said.

Both Ralph and Clara looked at him in surprise. He seemed blandly intent on being of service. Ralph had the feeling that Montrose was playing a game with him. The man's impeccable courtesy rang too false. Clara looked pleadingly at Ralph as if begging him to say something in her defense.

"When you feel rested..." Ralph's voice trailed off like a tattered ribbon.

The indignity of it fired Clara with such energy that she clambered out of the chair and stomped toward the door, mumbling resentfully as she went.

Montrose wound his watch. "You must be more decisive—with the help, that is."

Now what did he mean by that? Just how much did Montrose know and what did he suspect? Ralph studied him as he went behind the desk and took a bottle of clear liquid from the wall safe and poured two glasses half full.

"The *Señor* could use a little something to drink, maybe, before his dinner?" Smiling, he picked up one glass and urged it into Ralph's hand.

Ralph accepted the glass and drained its contents with one gulp, the liquid fire searing its way down the length of his gullet. His empty stomach sponged up the alcohol eagerly and he found himself weak and breathless.

"For one who is not accustomed to it, you drink this much too fast." Montrose refilled the glass. "It is better that you sip slowly and give the body a chance to feel its way with the native flower." His voice had become silky and insinuating, almost hypnotic, with a strange, Oriental deference in its tone.

Ralph held the second drink close to his face and stared down into it. He knew the stuff was potent. He always knew when to stop though, and besides, anything that pipsqueak Montrose could drink, he could double.

"Okay," he said, "I'll try it slow. I'll make believe it's brandy." He brought the glass up to his nostrils and inhaled the sweet, delicate aroma. Then he put his lips to the rim and tasted a drop on the tip of his tongue. Uncontrollably he bolted the rest.

"You're not learning very well." Montrose's voice had a regretful note that went well with his subtle touch of irony. He refilled Ralph's glass.

"Don't worry," Ralph said, "I'm learning plenty." He found a chair and sat down, cupping the glass protectively between his palms. The lights in the room suddenly seemed brighter to him. He stared up at the chandelier where he saw spinning discs of violet and orange, red and green and other colors whose names he didn't know. They circled and danced around the bulbs.

Dimly, far in the back of his mind, he kept saying to himself, "I mustn't get drunk... I mustn't get drunk. This is deliberate and I don't know why... so hang on, boy, and just don't get drunk. Hang on for all you've got."

When Montrose approached him with the bottle again, Ralph put his hand over the rim of the glass and shook his head. "No more," he mumbled. "Had 'nough."

The clerk leaned close to him and examined his face and eyes. He nodded. "Yes, *Señor*, you have had enough." Smiling, he poured the remaining contents of his own glass back into the bottle but Ralph did not notice. And he scarcely recognized Clara when she returned with a heavy wicker basket swinging from one plump arm. Montrose motioned for her to set it down on a low table that held old magazines and filthy ashtrays. As she did so, her glance fell upon Ralph and she stared at him unbelievingly and then shook her head sadly.

"How could you?" she asked, glaring contemptuously at Montrose. "And why?"

"You can leave now," he said to her coldly.

"The police will get you yet." She turned and stormed out of the lobby.

Ralph tried desperately to focus on the basket. He remembered that it held food—food for Alison. Alison's dinner. She would be waiting for it. He must take it to her right away. He leaned forward in the chair, intent on standing up. At the third effort, he succeeded. The basket seemed miles away, barely visible to his tired and aching eyes. He began to cough chokingly and Montrose rushed forward with a glass of cold water. As if from a great distance a voice reached him, feebly penetrating the wads of cotton batting that had settled in his ears.

"Let me hand you the basket, *Señor*," Montrose moved the basket from the table and slipped the handle over Ralph's outstretched arm.

The room was very large, the floor undulating like the sea, but Ralph knew what he must do. Cross the miles, the swaying miles, to the stairway at the other end and then climb, climb straight up to nowhere.

An idea came to him that seemed born of sheer inspiration. It would solve all of his problems. He would crawl. He held the basket out stiffly in front of him but his knees were limp, like melted cheese, and suddenly he was sitting on the floor, the basket beyond his reach. Painfully he maneuvered himself to his hands and knees and began the long voyage to the door and the stairs beyond.

Pushing the basket ahead of him with his head lowered, his chin nearly touching the carpet as he moved, he jerked forward, inching his way along, humping and straightening out like a caterpillar. Montrose watched with an amused smile playing about his lips and slowly followed.

When Ralph reached the stairs, he sat down on the floor for a moment and stared bleakly at the mountain rising above him. He shoved the basket, then himself, up to the first step. Then to the next. At last he reached the first landing where he sat down for a rest. Montrose touched his arm.

"Perhaps the *Señor* would like to retire for the night?" he suggested. "Perhaps the *Señor* is tired?"

What was the man saying? That he should stop now, retire? Foggily Ralph shook his head. He couldn't be tired. He had to get there. Never mind where. Just there. Again he began his tedious journey, and when the second landing was in sight, Montrose again touched his arm.

"*Señor,* there is no place for you up here. Your bed has been prepared in your room. Allow me to guide you." And he took Ralph's arm, attempting to lead him back to the first landing.

The insistent touch of the clammy fingers warned Ralph that he had little time left. Little time and little strength. He couldn't waste himself on this puny creature. He would have to run the rest of the way. He clutched the bannister and pulled himself to his feet. Montrose clung to his arm and Ralph shook him off, shoving him backward down the stairs with his other arm. Montrose toppled into a somersault and Ralph took the chance to float, to fly, it seemed, and somehow he was on the second landing.

He squinted down the hallway and fixed his eyes on the door. Alison's door. For a second he stared at it and then, with a final burst of bravado, he cut loose from the bannister and headed full speed down the hall, the wicker basket bouncing and gurgling at his side.

As if by magic, he suddenly found himself standing in front of the coveted door. Its panels of sparkling lights flashed and scattered wildly before his eyes. He pushed his fist through the glare and, meeting with solid substance, he rapped loudly.

No answer.

He braced a shoulder hard against the door and shoved with all his strength. He heard the latch give and felt the door click open a scant quarter of an inch. He pushed his weight against it heavily and it gave way before his bulk.

He heard a woman's scream.

As he catapulted head-first into the room, his eyes riveted on the bed. The two women lying together on it—naked and locked in a close embrace—struggled apart, wide-eyed in horror and shock.

One of them was Alison.

The other one resembled Alison but was older, with streaks of silver in her thick, black hair.

CHAPTER FOUR

RALPH GRADUALLY awoke and sensed that he was lying on something soft. He kept his eyes closed tight and waited for his head to shrink to a size that he could handle. His body felt like a helium-inflated toy that would have floated up and away if his lead feet were not anchoring it to the bed.

He lay perfectly still, listening for a sound that would indicate his surroundings. He heard the far-off dripping of a faucet. He blinked his eyelids open and waited painfully for his eyes to focus. The ornate curves of the iron bedstead were like those of his own but he knew instinctively that he was not in his own room. Dizzily he turned his head from right to left and tried to focus again. Then he saw a pair of slim legs dressed in powder blue slacks and crossed at the ankles. The feet were bound in mahogany leather sandals.

He recognized the toes, the high rounded instep, the slender ankles, and he tried to smile. His eyes followed the graceful, relaxed line of her body up to her face. She had just lit a cigarette and it still clung to the corner of her mouth. Her right eye squinted behind the rising cloud of smoke.

"Hi," she said, and the cigarette bobbed.

He grunted something that he meant for a hello. The sound of his voice reverberated through his head and he groaned. She sat quietly in the chair, watching him in her usual careless way.

After a while he managed to raise himself on his elbows. He pushed the pillow against the headboard and leaned back, careful not to jar his aching head. He wondered where he was. How had he gotten here? And what was she doing here? She seemed calm and serene but he sensed an uneasiness in the air. Certainly she was not here because of concern about his well-being. Dimly he knew there was something different about her but his mind could not quite identify it. Nevertheless, he felt that he had the advantage and that it would be wise to stall for time until he could figure out precisely what that advantage was.

"Well," she said, taking the cigarette out of her mouth and flicking an ash to the floor. "You're beginning to look alive."

"Camouflage." He noted that the light coming through the window was that of rising sun. So it was morning. But where the hell was last night? He continued with a wry smile, "If you'll tell me where my clothes are, I'll try to go through with the act."

"Sorry, friend." She stood up and went to the window. "You messed yourself up last night. Your suit's being cleaned."

As he watched her cross the room, he struggled with the fragment of a memory—and then it all came back to him. In dawning horror he cradled his head in his hands, frantically sorting and assessing the remembered abomination of the night before.

He thought he would be sick again. Alison, his Alison, a...a...? His mind balked. It couldn't be true. She was his, and had been his with complete and utter surrender. She belonged to him! Yet the fact remained that he had glimpsed her in the embrace of a woman.

If he had found her with another man, it might have been easier to understand, but this! How could he cope with it? He could bash in another man's face, beat him to a pulp, but what could he do to a woman? And what kind of a hold did that woman have on Alison? How strong was it? How long had it been in existence? How would he break it?

That the hold could be broken, he did not doubt for a moment. After all, he had evidence of Alison's essential health, of her deep and fiery need for the male.

With a sudden, raging desire to do violence, he pushed away the flimsy cover and swung his feet off the bed. He grabbed the bedpost to steady himself. He had to get out fast, while he was still responsible for what he might do or say. It wasn't too far to his room. The floor was shaky beneath his feet but he reached the door before he felt her hand on his arm.

"Don't go yet. Sit down." The hand closed over his. "There are a few things you don't know about and I think it's time I told you."

"Later."

"But it wasn't all his fault."

Ralph hesitated. "Whose fault?"

"The clerk's," she said.

He turned around and leaned heavily against the door. "I'm listening."

"Well, the truth is," she said carefully, "he only did what I told him to do." She led him away from the door and sat him down on the edge of the bed. "Oh, don't look so shocked. I hadn't meant for him to dope you. I just wanted him to detain you for a little while, long enough for my aunt and myself . . . well, until we could get a plane back to the States. It was for your own good, or I meant it to be, because you seemed so involved." Her voice was soothing, persuasive.

"Involved?" he echoed. "You don't understand. I love you, Alison, and I want you—for keeps. Who is this aunt, anyway?"

The girl got up and took a few rapid steps across the room and back again. He saw that she was annoyed but, for some reason, was keeping a tight rein on herself. She stopped in front of him.

"You're being difficult." Her voice was taut.

"You mean the lady who met you at the pier? Nice-looking woman. I'd be very glad to meet her."

He sat there waiting for her to slap his face, to stamp her feet or to throw a tantrum. It would be nice to see her violent, human.

But instead she calmed herself and managed the ghost of a smile. "You'll meet her," she said, "but not while you're dressed like that."

He realized that Alison was not going to be honest with him. She never would be, so long as she was under the influence of that woman. And she could lie much too well. What mattered now was that she was no longer trying to lose him, get rid of him.

"So why don't you go back to sleep till your things are ready?" she suggested. "I'll bring them in to you myself. Or would you like some bacon and eggs and coffee first?"

"You're right. I could use some more sleep." He got back into the bed and stretched out. "The food can wait until I come down for it."

She pulled the cover up to his chin. "Dream nice things," she said.

He closed his eyes and listened for the door to close behind her. He waited for the time he figured it would take her to reach the stairs and go down or to go into another room somewhere.

Then he climbed out of bed. Silently he crossed the room to the door. He turned the knob slowly and in bare feet went quietly down the hall. His stomach was empty and sore and in desperate need of coffee but he reached his room and climbed into his swimming trunks. They were still a little damp around the waist and a shiver ran through him. A quick glance showed that the gear on the floor had not been touched, nor had the suitcase.

He took a cake of soap from the bathroom and went down to the lobby. The desk clerk's elbow lay on the arm of his usual reading chair. Moving soundlessly across the room until he stood behind the chair, Ralph brought his hand sharply across Montrose's face, forcing the soap into his mouth.

"Stand up," Ralph whispered. His palm pressed flat against the man's lips, mashing them back to the teeth. With the other hand, he grabbed the back of Montrose's jacket and pulled him to his feet. Montrose's hands flayed the air and Ralph could hear him swallowing and choking to prevent the soap from slipping down his throat. He did not try to struggle free but got to his feet and moved ahead of Ralph.

Montrose found himself being pushed up the stairs and into Ralph's room. Then Ralph threw the man forward against the wall and twisted his arm behind his back in a punishing hammerlock. His eyes stared blindly at the ceiling, his lips were frozen in an agonized grimace. Ralph forced him into the bathroom and kicked the door closed, then he turned the hot water on full force and shoved the other's head under the steam. The soap came spitting out of his mouth and plopped into the water.

"All of it," Ralph rasped, shaking him hard. "Every damned thing you know."

Gagging and spitting, Montrose struggled backward from the steaming water. Ralph held him steady.

"Can't—" He started to retch, this thin body convulsing. Ralph felt the neck grow clammy.

The body sagged, the chin thudded sickeningly against the edge of the sink. Ralph released his grasp and watched the body fall. It lay still on the floor, blood welling from between the swollen lips.

After a few minutes Montrose stirred and began to moan. Ralph put a handkerchief to the bloody face, hauled the man up by the jacket, dragged him into the other room and let him drop into a chair. With a trembling hand, Montrose held the reddening cloth to his mouth.

"Talk!" Ralph stood over him with clenched fists, ready to pummel the quivering body.

Montrose took away the handkerchief to speak but no sound would come. Ralph grabbed his lapels and jerked him forward. The clerk shook his head and put his hands against Ralph's naked shoulders.

"No, no, please ... I speak."

Ralph pushed him back into the chair and a sigh escaped the blown-up lips. He put the cloth against his mouth and winced. Then he swallowed painfully. "Water!" he gasped.

Even in his fury, Ralph realized that Montrose would not be able to say much in this condition. He pulled the handkerchief from the man's grasp, strode into the bathroom and shut off the hot water. Turning on the other tap, he thrust the blood-soaked cloth into the stream of cold water. Then he filled a glass with tepid water and took glass and cloth back to Montrose.

Gratefully Montrose took the glass. Some of the water spilled down the front of his white suit. He patted his lips with the wet handkerchief, then put his tongue into the glass. His face crinkled with revulsion as the water mixed with blood and soap. He lapped some of the water into his mouth, then spit it back into the glass.

"Get to it," Ralph warned.

Montrose relaxed limply against the chair. "Not my fault, *Señor*." The words came thickly. "I only do what the *Señoritas* say."

"Which one?"

"Young one. She say hold you here. She give me money. Much money."

"How much?"

"Thousand dollars." As Ralph stood speechless beside him, Montrose lifted the glass to his face and again lapped his tongue in the water.

"Then why didn't they leave?" Ralph demanded.

Montrose shook his head slowly. *"Quien sabe?"*

Ralph snatched the glass from the limp fingers and threw the water into his face. "I said, why didn't they go?"

Water dripped from the clerk's nose. He lifted his sleeve to it and trembled with pain as he grazed his lips. "I made a mistake. Not make you sleep soon enough. You reach the second floor. You found out …" His voice trailed off.

"But they could have gone anyway."

"No. The *Señorita,* the older one, she thinks with the knowledge you may cause trouble. The pretty one laughs and says you are not interested in business but the older one, she does not believe. She is *segura* you will cause trouble."

"Business?"

Montrose had talked too much and the blood began to flow freely from his mouth. He pressed his sleeve to his lips and looked from the glass in Ralph's hand to his eyes. His expression was pleading.

Ralph refilled the glass but held it out of Montrose's grasp. "Tell me about the business," he said.

"They do business here to buy the *isla* from the government. Island that the young *Señorita* visits. They will buy the island and build a big resort there—for ladies *solamente.* Rich ladies. To come from all over the world, and—and relax with each other. Do as they please, with nobody to look on or say no."

"How do you know all this?"

"I have been agent for the *Señoritas* a long time," he said. "Ever since they began to come here for vacations—and privacy. They pay me well for small *negocios,* and they trust me."

Ralph handed him the glass of water. So that was why he, Ralph, had found Alison on the sand. She had been looking the place over, investigating. But why had she returned after that first day to spend all that time there with him? He thought about it carefully and could think of no reason other than himself. She must have enjoyed him and decided to give in for a moment to her pleasure. But what was the bond that now kept her tied to the older woman? Habit? Fear? He could not believe that it was simply one of free choice.

He did not want to ask too many questions. Montrose was on territory now where he could say all he wanted to without having to prove a thing. Ralph crossed the room and lay down on the bed, his arms folded behind his head.

"All right," he said without looking at Montrose. "Get the hell out of here."

The little man stared at him. "Go?"

"Yes. Scram."

Montrose rose unsteadily to his feet and lurched toward the door.

"When the *Señoritas* ask," Ralph said, pressing the heels of his hands into his eyes, "tell them I'm in here." He scarcely heard the door close before he fell asleep.

The remains of the drug were still working on him.

It was nearly dark when he awoke to the cries of birds clustered above the fishing boats that were bringing in the day's catch. He felt a gnawing emptiness in his stomach and flung himself out of bed. The floor seemed to wobble beneath his feet and his legs were rubbery, as though he hadn't used them for six months. He found his clothes hanging on a hook behind the door, neatly cleaned and pressed.

When he went downstairs, the lobby had an air of calm. He spotted Montrose, his face covered with bandages, his eyes closed, reclining on a sofa. Ignoring him, Ralph went behind the counter. Two cable envelopes lay near the phone, face down. He flipped them over and saw that one was addressed to him and the other to Maxine Carpentier. He ripped open his own and glanced over it quickly. GRAND FOLLOWING. WHERE'S MY STORY? ED.

A moment of conscience touched Ralph with that old, familiar sense of duty. Ed was getting the dirty end of the stick this time. Ralph tore the cable to shreds and crammed the scraps into his pocket. If he let Ed down it would be tantamount to blacklisting himself as a photo-journalist. Nobody would give him another assignment. Still, what the hell difference did that make now?

He went over to Montrose. The man had been pretending to sleep. As Ralph watched, he could see the twitching of the clerk's eyelids. "Fork over twenty-five bucks," Ralph said evenly. He stood over Montrose, waiting, menacing.

Montrose's hand crept slowly into his pants pocket and emerged with a five-dollar bill. He shook his head and spread his hands helplessly. Ralph snatched the bill.

"You can tell the *Señoritas* that I have gone for breakfast."

He turned his back on the man and strolled across the lobby and out into the twilight. The day was still warm enough to make his head begin a monotonous thudding. His breakfast consisted of fish sticks, black coffee and, a shot of native rum. His confidence returned after the rum and his step was surer. He was convinced that he could win Alison away from Maxine.

Instead of going back up the hill to the hotel, he turned toward the water, searching the line of boats bobbing at anchor, hoping to find the *Jim Boy*. The cabin craft should be easy to spot among the small sailboats and clumsy fishing boats. But seek as he might, Ralph could not find it. He swore at himself for not having learned the name of the giant skipper.

Ralph headed back toward town and stopped in the first of the native bars that he came to. He bought a pack of cigarettes with his last piece of change. A fat man sat crosslegged on the bar, plucking a sad tune on his guitar, his black mustache drooping like a weeping willow, his eyes bloodshot and sad. Ralph sat down on one of the rickety stools and ordered a drink.

The waiter looked at Montrose's five-dollar bill lying flat on the bar and set the bottle before Ralph. He tipped it over and filled the glass mug. He took two more drinks before he picked up the bottle, set it on the bar in front of the man with the guitar, got his change and walked out.

Dusk had painted the sky with a purple mist. He sighed and wondered what had become of the boat and its native skipper. Then he headed for the hotel, determined now to meet Maxine and get down to cases.

CHAPTER FIVE

RALPH had not gone fifteen feet up the hill before he saw the cart jouncing along the narrow pathway toward him. In it the silhouettes of three familiar figures rocked with the bumps of the road. He stepped quickly out of their sight and flattened himself against the shadow side of a boulder as they passed him.

He had expected them to be going toward the dock. He was surprised to see that when the wagon reached the flat land near the water, it turned to the left and continued along the ocean's edge, following the rough path leading out of Kinderman. He left his hiding place and hurried to keep up with them.

He soon realized that he would not be able to follow long on foot. He was becoming winded. A sharp pain jabbed his side. Either he would have to go back to the hotel and let them go on without him or else persuade them to take him along.

He cupped his hands to his mouth and shouted. Two of the three heads turned to look at him. The third one, holding itself as proudly as ever, faced firmly ahead but he saw it nod ever so slightly and the donkey cart ground to a creaking halt.

He took his time. When he reached them, he swung himself easily up beside Montrose and, turning to the back seat, inclined his head and said in his most pleasant manner, "Good evening, ladies."

Alison, still wearing the blue slacks, her hands resting lightly in her lap, said calmly, "Maxine, this is Ralph Thayer, the famous photographer. I'm sure you've seen his work. Ralph, meet my aunt, Maxine Carpentier."

The woman looked at him directly and evenly. "Yes, I'm quite familiar with his photography. Recently he had some things reproduced in *La Soiree*. Is that not correct, Mr. Thayer?" Her voice was as rich and resonant as a man's.

Ralph nodded, caught momentarily off guard. If they had met at a social function, he knew he probably would have liked this woman. Undoubtedly, in her own setting, she would prove a person of wit and intelligence. Her body appeared to have the strength and suppleness of immense vitality. Strange, he thought, that he could find this twisted woman attractive.

Montrose, obviously in pain and making no attempt to conceal it, steered the donkey around such bumps in the road as he could see. Ralph ignored him and sat facing the two women, fascinated and yet disturbed by the resemblance between them. He noticed that the older woman tilted her nose in aversion to his alcoholic breath. He lit a cigarette.

"You enjoy the coral islands?" the woman asked casually. Her eyes glinted with a bitter irony, barbing a seemingly innocent question.

"Yes. I have come here for many years to vacation. There is one island in particular that interests me." He met her challenge with his own. Beside him, he heard Montrose swallow. "In fact," Ralph continued, "it was on that island that I met Alison."

The woman's lips tightened at his use of the girl's first name.

"Yes," Alison said. She brushed away a lock of hair that had blown into her eyes. "And really, he swims almost as well as Mars. Perhaps we'll be able to persuade him to stay on and help us."

Both women looked at him steadily and suddenly he knew what was expected of him. He shrugged.

"I'm willing to do whatever I can for you both."

Alison grinned with obvious amusement. Maxine nodded at the acceptance of her terms.

They joggled on. Along the water's edge, twisted trees threw deep shadows across the rocks, and high in the branches birds ruffled their feathers and settled on their perches to sleep. The day's heat had turned to a crisp coolness marked by a breeze that nipped the ears and whipped the cheeks with a tang of salt spray. Half a thin moon rode high in the indigo sky. Only the sound of the creaking wheels broke the night's stillness and in the distance Ralph could still see a few of Kinderman's lights. On this road they could not possibly travel the thirty miles to the next town. He turned to face ahead, but saw nothing through the darkness of the night.

He would not give them the satisfaction of asking where they were going. He wondered vaguely if Alison had told the woman anything of what had happened between them. Even if she had not, Maxine Carpentier was too intelligent, too astute, not to be curious. And, he thought, probably too possessive and jealous.

The evening mist had settled heavily on his face and hands and soaked through his clothes to his skin when Montrose finally picked up the reins and pulled the old animal to a halt. Ralph glanced around but saw nothing to indicate a stopping place. He jumped out quickly and offered his hand to the women.

Alison jumped out lightly on her side of the cart but Maxine remained seated, leaving Ralph standing in the road like a useless statue. Angrily, he shoved his hands into his pockets.

Stepping without hesitation among the rocks, Alison moved down to the water and sat on a flat stone. Ralph followed and joined her but remained standing. Above the lapping of the water against the shore, he heard the faint sound of an engine.

"The *Jim Boy?*" he asked.

"Yes."

"You know," he said, "I don't like to ask questions but it would be nice if somebody let me in on what's going on." He tried to assume a bantering tone.

"All right, you poor thing." She sat facing the ocean, her eyes turned to the water, her legs pulled up tight, her chin resting on her knees. "You wanted to stay with me for a while. Well, you're getting your chance. Some of our friends are coming in to look at the island and okay it for construction. You can help me guide them, if all goes as it should. And you can stay on while the place is being built. Then afterward you can serve as a sort of general escort and public relations man. Take care of the things that men are good for," she said. Her last sentence had a double edge.

Together they waited as the sound of the engine grew louder. When they could see the shadow of the boat, she took his hand and pulled herself upward.

Hardly realizing that he spoke his thoughts aloud, he asked, "Why are you so eager?"

In the darkness he felt her move close to him and touch her fingertips to his chin. "You mistake me," she said softly. Her voice held a hint of tenderness that he had never noticed in it before. "It is only the habit of thinking that tomorrow will be better than today. If you were a gambler, you would understand."

His arms reached out to hold her but she turned quickly and began to pick her way down to the line of beach that penciled along the shore. He followed her and they stood together in silence listening to the splash of the lowered rowboat and the creaking of oarlocks.

In a few minutes the giant skipper leaped out of the dinghy and dragged its prow up on the sand. He approached and stood before Alison.

"Good evenin', miss," he said. Although he held his voice to a whisper, Ralph could tell that it was as big and deep as the man himself.

"Good evening, Noah. Miss Carpentier is waiting on the road. Go help her down, please."

Without another word, the man leaped up the rocks as agilely as a goat.

"Noah is our man of all work. So was his father. We used to have lots of servants—but not any more." She spoke half to Ralph, half to herself.

Soon Noah appeared, carrying the woman in his arms as easily as though she were a child. He waded with her to the boat where he set her gently on a seat. Then he waited patiently for Ralph and Alison to join them. Alison pulled off her sandals and rolled up the legs of her slacks. Ralph followed her example and in minutes they were being rowed toward the cabin cruiser.

They pulled up beside the *Jim Boy* and one by one they ascended the rope ladder. Ralph noticed that despite her tight skirt Maxine climbed with remarkable ease.

He was thinking guiltily about the battered Montrose painfully making his way alone back to the hotel when his thoughts were jolted to a sudden halt by an abrupt confusion of voices as three women rushed from the cabin to greet them. In the mingling of arms and chatter, he found himself forgotten and alone. He moved over to the rail and watched the scene curiously.

Noah, at the wheel, opened the throttle wide, brought the boat about and headed out to sea. When the greetings had quieted and one of the three figures had left to attend to a fishing pole, he heard Alison ask:

"Did you folks remember to bring something to drink?"

A tall person, leaning against the railing opposite Ralph, said, "My goodness, yes. Just switch on the lights and you'll see. This darkness is such a bore. I really don't see why you insist on such secrecy."

A hatchlight was lit and Ralph saw that the speaker was an attractive woman with slightly waved and prematurely white hair pulled back into a severe bun so that it appeared almost cropped. She wore black tailored slacks and a tight-fitting crewneck sweater that flattered her tall thinness with a sporty air of youth. Actually, she was probably well past thirty. Her face seemed familiar to Ralph, although at the moment he could not place it.

"Without this secrecy you think so foolish," Maxine said, settling herself into a yacht chair, "we would soon be the favorite subject of every newspaper in the world. Much scandal, which we hardly need, would descend upon us as well as difficulties of a more concrete nature."

"Oh, Max, for heaven's sakes. This isn't Soviet Russia." The woman at the rail tossed her head in annoyance.

Then Ralph suddenly recognized her. Lillian Marsh, ex-wife of the diplomat. He had often seen her. In the newsreels, at the christening of ships or when boarding planes. And if he remembered correctly she had once been a singer.

A girl in leather shorts went over to Max and put a hand on her arm. "Anyhow, what about getting started? We've been waiting for ages." She widened her blue eyes and they seemed to light up as if there were bulbs inside them. The long blond bangs, soft as baby's hair, lifted slightly in the breeze. Even as she reached for a highball, the girl reserved her smile for Max alone.

As Max gently but firmly shrugged her off, a loud scuffling of feet and a trumpeting of victory came from the cabin deck, along with the *whirr* of a reel being wound in furiously.

"I got you! *Yeeouwhee!*"

A flat, struggling fish whipped through the air, missing the blonde girl by inches, and landed on the deck, slapping furiously and spattering everyone with cold drops of sea water.

"Oh, Judy, for heaven's sake," came Lillian's distraught voice.

Judy bounded down the ladder, her pleasant round face beaming with excitement, her cropped, curly hair tousled and falling over her forehead. She was wearing a gray sweatshirt, boxer trunks and sneakers, all of them splashed and dripping. She waved the fishing pole through the air like a whip, bringing the fish off the deck and dangerously close to Lillian.

Alison called out, "Put Moby Dick away and come have a drink with us."

Judy pulled back on the rod, caught the fish in her hand and removed it lovingly from the hook. Her fingers were still in the gills when she caught sight of Ralph near the light.

"Hi," she said.

Ralph smiled back at the brown eyes that were regarding him with friendly good nature. "Hello."

He found himself being examined suddenly by three pairs of inquisitive eyes, one pair friendly, one pair empty of any expression and the third, from across the deck, frankly appraising. Three more females to worry about—as if Alison and Maxine were not enough! He felt decidedly uncomfortable but he stood calmly and let them stare.

Alison said to him, "How did I manage to forget about you?" She brought him a drink and stood beside him, deliberately linking her arm in his. "Lillian, Susie, Judy—this is Ralph Thayer. He will be your badge of propriety and respectability. Please try to be natural so he can learn how to conduct himself among us." As she spoke, her glance flitted quickly from face to face, avoiding only Maxine's.

The woman was staring grimly out at the churning water. Her profile was tilted up as proudly as a ship's prow, mutely protesting the indignity caused her by Ralph's presence. For a moment he almost pitied her, but he knew that she would have to try, in some subtle way, to destroy him, for he was the man she would have liked to be. A woman as proud as she was could not exist passively in such close proximity with the living reminder of her incompleteness.

Alison released his arm and went across the deck to blonde Susie, who had finished one drink and was pouring herself another, consisting of straight whiskey up to the rim of the glass. With her lips to the brim, the blue eyes looked out upon the world as innocently as those of a child taking its afternoon milk. Alison took the glass away from her and sat down, pulling the girl down beside her and speaking in tones so low that Ralph could not overhear.

"Maybe you'd like to come fishing with me? I get kinda sick of looking at these old buzzards sometimes." Judy laughed. She pulled at her sweatshirt and looked down at it. "Including myself," she said with decision, "so maybe it wouldn't be such a hot idea for you at that."

The girl stood a chunky five feet five. The top of her head barely reached Ralph's shoulder. When she looked up at him, he saw laugh wrinkles around the corners of her eyes. She could have been fifteen, she could have been thirty. Ralph liked her immediately, liked her openness, her carefree manner.

"Come on," he said. "Let's fish." He found it easy to trust her. She seemed like a kid brother just home from camp. "You got an extra line up there?"

She made a light sound of annoyance. "Damn, I forgot about that. But use mine for a while and I'll kibitz. Then we can switch."

They clambered up the companionway to the wide, canted deck atop the cabin, slippery with the wetness of salt spray. Mars lay curled up, nose between paws, near the can of bait.

"Sit still while I bait your hook." Judy placed the rod in his hands and he held it, sitting cross-legged on the deck.

"Okay." Judy stepped back. "Cast."

Ralph pulled the pole backward, then whipped it forward and heard the line whiz out into the darkness and plop into the ocean. Judy sat down beside him, crossing her legs and leaning forward with her elbows propped on her knees. "You know what?"

"What?"

"That girl mixes a very strong drink," she said, nodding solemnly. "I can feel my tongue beginning to swell already. Like a soggy old sponge. Now if it was beer ... You like beer?" she asked suddenly.

"So-so." He shrugged. He could smell the faint, lingering odor of after-shave lotion on the back of her neck. "But in the natural state I go mostly for Scotch on the rocks."

"She does too, your friend. It's a wonder that lass can swim two feet. But who am I to talk?" She reached out to adjust the pole in his hands. "You have to be careful to keep the line from going too slack. You miss them that way. Of course, this sort of thing takes a lot of intuition, too. Sorta like women. Me, I catch more finny ones than furry ones," she sighed, "but I sure can lecture like I was a real authority on the subject."

Ralph took the crumpled cigarette she offered him and leaned forward to accept a light. "Well, then, lecture me this, if you please."

She waved a hand. "Anything."

"Why do attractive and apparently wealthy women have to trek down here to this godforsaken place when there are so many spots catering to them back in so-called civilization?" His cigarette, damp, went out and he reached for hers to get another light. "You folks hardly seem the anti-social type."

"Excepting one," she added. It seemed almost sacrilegious for them to be laughing at Max behind her back but they both found it a relief.

"Anyway," she continued, "it isn't so much a question of our sociability. Max long ago decided that there should be a place where we would be free to let our hair down—those of us who have any, that is." She rubbed her own short hair and wrinkled her nose. "We wanted to be free from graft, too. There comes a time for those like us when we want to buy something more with our money than just a zoo with a good strong fence around it. We get tired of making compromises with life. And why the hell should we have to if we can afford to do something about it? Now that we've found the ideal location, we're going to build the best resort that money and influence can buy. It'll give us the closest thing to freedom that we can achieve."

"And where does Alison fit into all this?" Ralph asked casually.

A smile inflated Judy's chubby cheeks. "You like her?" she asked. "I guess we all do. Well, that's a hard one to answer. Her aunt, Max, raised her, you know. She's lived with Max most of her life. Max has Alison's money tied up until she's twenty-one, which won't be for another year or two. Besides, they're really attached to each other. There's a strong family resemblance between them and it makes for a kind of mutual admiration."

She paused for a drag on her cigarette and then went on. "But the time will come when Alison will outgrow all of this. Right now, since everything bores her, she indulges in the fringe pleasures just to keep from falling asleep, so to speak. How do you like that," she laughed, "me calling myself a fringe pleasure? Anyway, she's been catered to all her life by somebody or other. You can't expect her to sit up and suddenly start entertaining herself, can you? Not when there's always someone else around to do it for her."

Ralph nodded a little grimly, knowing that what Judy told him was true.

She put a hand on his shoulder. "Whatever your troubles may be, Ralph, just remember that that baby down there is no happier than you are," she said. "There, I told you I could lecture."

From the deck below came the strains of a slow arrangement of *My Funny Valentine*. They looked down and saw that Lillian was dancing with Susie. Their bodies were pressed tightly together and, as they moved in time with the music, their thighs remained in contact. The blonde girl leaned her cheek against the older woman's ear.

Out of Ralph's presence, Maxine had relaxed a little. Gently she entwined her fingers in Alison's hair as the girl sat beside her. Ralph decided to remain silent and stay where he was so that he could watch them. He gripped the fishing pole as if he wished it were Maxine's throat.

"Easy, boy." Judy flipped her cigarette into the wind. "You let the wrong things get you."

"Wrong, hell! A girl like that shouldn't be coerced into this—this sickness."

"You don't give Alison credit for making the decision herself?" she asked easily.

"Wasn't it you who just finished saying something about a lifelong influence?"

"Ah, Ralph, like all men, you imagine your influence is necessarily better."

Ralph could not take his eyes from Maxine's hand. He wanted to break it off at the wrist. The fingers caressed Alison's cheek and then slipped around to the back of her slim neck. Alison looked up at Maxine and smiled tenderly. Resentment flashed hot inside of him. In his anger he half arose. As a wave careened the boat, his feet slid out from under him on the slippery deck and he crashed over the edge and down to the duckboards below, landing with a thud on his back. A wild pain tore through him.

Lillian and Susie stopped dancing and bent over him. Susie kept asking, "Are you hurt? Are you hurt?"

Shaking his head, he rose slowly and painfully to his feet. "I'm all right," he said. "Please." He blushed with humiliation.

Catching Maxine's glance, he saw in her eyes a quiet satisfaction. He knew it would have been all right with her if he had killed himself.

By this time Judy had clambered down from the cabin deck. "Let's have a look," she said.

"Please, Judy. I'm all right."

"It's perfectly cricket," Lillian assured him. "She's a doctor, if you can believe it."

"Ex-doctor," Judy corrected her. "Some gal once thought she was going to blackmail me, but I decided to be stubborn." She poked her strong fingers around his spine and made him bend in various undignified positions. "You'll live," she said. "It's just a jolt. Next time, I'll try to trip you up a little bit more artistically."

He looked at her quickly but could see no sign that she was making fun of him. She was merely trying to save his face. He felt that he had finally found himself a friend.

The skipper, Noah, forgotten during the trip, suddenly made his presence felt by throttling the engine.

"Are we almost there?" Maxine's voice cut through the air like a saber.

"A while yet," the huge pilot replied. "We have to go slow around here. Many reefs in this water."

The radio, a large Telefunken, muttered something in a guttural German and began a lively version of *Begin the Beguine*. Ralph wanted to shut off the thing or heave it into the water. But Susie, apparently addicted to dancing as well as alcohol, fell on Lillian again and they began to sway.

His spinal column felt as if it had been hacked from top to bottom with a sharp ax and he looked around for a soft place to sit. The only thing that would serve the purpose was the hassock at Maxine's feet but he did not want to be near her. She was utterly repulsive to him and the thought of her hand caressing Alison outraged every nerve in his body.

He turned toward the taffrail and sat down on the deck. In a moment, however, his pain became unbearable and he got up to take a long drink from the bottle in a basket nearby. When he put back the bottle and turned again to the stern rails, he saw that Alison was dragging the hassock toward him.

"Here," she said. "Try this." She stood beside him and he saw moonlight floating in her hair. He wanted to bury his face in the graceful tresses but instead he sat down heavily on the hassock. He sighed and leaned his forehead against her thigh.

He wound his arms around her knees and held her tight. He looked up the length of her slim body and then pulled her down next to him. She kneeled on the deck beside him and his arms fell heavily around her shoulders.

"Alison," he said wearily, "Alison, let's go home, just you and me. How about it?"

Gently she loosened his fingers, then held his wrists and backed out of his reach. "Now you're being funny," she said with a patient laugh.

"Alison, don't play with me. I'm serious. Let's just you and me get the hell out of here."

He knew that she thought he was drunk, but he wasn't. He was confused—and tired. So tired. And he ached. If she would just be reasonable, everything would be all right. If she would just. . . .

"Is he passing out there?" This was Maxine's voice and it made him livid with anger.

His head whipped around. "No, he's not passing out here," he aped her. He jumped to his feet and defiantly put his arm around Alison's waist. "And what's more, he's not drunk either."

With a quick movement, he pulled her toward him with both hands and kissed her hard. His arms held her tight and he felt the soft flesh of her breasts crush against his chest. Her hands pushed at his shoulders, struggling to free herself. He held her fast, forcing her mouth open with his tongue. Suddenly she caught her breath, her body surged toward him, her tongue met his and she responded as eagerly as when first he had kissed her on their coral island.

Crack! He felt a sharp sting across his back, then another, and a blow that cut into his neck. Pain finally made him release her. He whirled away from her and caught a flick across his face. He put his hand up to protect his eyes.

"Are you quite calm now?" Maxine asked, her voice trembling with rage. She stood facing him, the fishing pole clenched tightly in her right hand, the left smoothing out her jacket. Breathing in gasps, her chin jutting forward, she dared him to defy her.

Alison had pulled herself away from him and was leaning against the rail, staring into the water. The others glared at him. Even Judy had lost her good humor for the moment. She stood belligerently with her feet apart, one fist on her hip, the nostrils of her short nose flaring with agitation.

Abruptly he turned his back on them, collapsed to the deck. He felt sick and strange and he bent out over the stem rails, heaving as though his insides were being torn from him. A clammy film spread over his body and he shivered uncontrollably. Then it was over and he lay there, alone and miserable, drained of all strength. His knees were limp and he sank slowly to the deck, his head against one of the lower bars. A throaty voice was singing *Smoke Gets In Your Eyes*.

He heard Lillian say, "They're all animals."

If there had been an escape, he would gladly have taken it, but he was trapped. He wanted to lie down and rest, to sleep if he could. The effects of that drug, the liquor, the fall on his back, these combined to provoke overwhelming weakness. He was dazed and muddled but of one thing he was certain. He never wanted to see any of them again, not even Alison.

For a while he let his imagination toy with the idea of shoving Maxine overboard. The thought quieted him and gradually he became strangely peaceful. He sighed and spread out full-length on the deck, listening to the rush of water against the sides of the boat. Occasionally the spray rose to bathe his face and finally he closed his eyes to rest.

Susie said cheerfully, "Well, let's all have another drink and just forget him."

"Maybe, if we're lucky, he'll roll over the side and slide down to a watery death," Lillian said. She turned to Maxine. "For heaven's sake, what's he doing with us anyway? I should think that if we needed a foil, at least you'd have picked a docile one."

"We didn't pick him at all," Maxine said impatiently. "He floundered into our room the other night and caught us at an embarrassing moment. There's a lot at stake here, and he knows too much to be trusted."

"You think he's going to tell someone? How utterly preposterous."

"You completely miss the point, old girl." Judy stood up and struck a wooden match with her fingernail. She held it out for Alison's cigarette.

"Whatever you may think, Lillian, we can't afford to take any chances." Maxine turned her head to look at Alison. "Besides, I have other reasons for keeping an eye on this man."

"My soul," breathed Susie.

"Well, I say the hell with it." Judy's voice returned to its usual bantering tone. "That poor guy's had enough tonight to keep him quiet for the rest of the year. Why don't we take him back to the mainland? We can drop him at Las Palmas, where he can go off about his own business and we'll be off about ours."

"It's not that easy, my friend. I cannot just dismiss the fact that he observed more than he should," said Maxine.

Alison sauntered over to take a look at Ralph. After a moment, she turned and motioned for Judy to join her. They stood beside him at the rail, looking down at his still body.

"Think he's all right?" Alison asked in a quiet voice. "He looks awfully pale to me."

"He just passed out, that's all," Judy said. "The poor guy. Your aunt really has it in for him, hasn't she?"

"Well, there's a lot more to it than she's telling, of course, but you know how it is, Judy," Alison said, looking at the girl and frowning slightly. "All my life she's been used to thinking that I belong exclusively to her. And now ... well, she's just plain jealous, I suppose." Alison sighed. "I don't know what to do. I really don't. What have I ever been able to do—about her?" She took the silver clasp from the back of her hair and let the wind move through the dark curls. The moonlight gleamed in her eyes.

"I don't know what you can do about her," Judy said, "but it seems to me that by this time a woman as smart as Max ought to know how things stand. After all, she's basically a sensible person even if it's a little hard to see it right now. I'm sure she wouldn't try to tie you up like this if it wasn't doing anybody any good."

Alison smiled and for a moment she closed her eyes. "You'd be surprised," she said. "And besides, it's no longer a question of being sensible, is it? It's been this way for so many years, practically since I can remember. To be honest, Judy, I don't know myself whether she's what I want or not. Nobody else has ever managed to keep me interested for very long. Oh, I don't know. Sometimes I think that if she didn't always have to be the boss—"

"When you're afraid of losing the one you love ..." Judy began but Alison interrupted her.

"You don't have to tell me, Judy. I know all about it," she said. "And now, on top of everything else, she's determined to give this character a hard time." She sighed. "Boy, are we going to have fun!"

Their voices penetrated the fog of Ralph's mind but he lay still with his eyes shut. He was through fighting for the night.

CHAPTER SIX

NOAH VEERED the *Jim Boy* sharply to the left and called out, "We're comin' in soon now."

His announcement excited the five women to a stir of activity. Susie found a comb and pulled it through her hair, then smoothed out the bangs. Lillian stood up to brush a few invisible specks from her slacks. Judy moved about quickly, gathering glasses. Maxine turned to watch the off-shore lights as they became visible, her strong hands gripping the rail, her nose tilted upward, all of her alert and alive.

Alison went over to Ralph and bent down to him. She patted his cheeks briskly and turned his head from side to side. "Come on, boy," she said. "Let's go."

He had not been asleep but he aroused himself with difficulty. The salt dampness had settled into his bruised bones. He grabbed a stanchion and, with teeth clenched, pulled himself to his feet.

"Say, what time is it?" he asked suddenly. But Alison had left him. She was standing beside Maxine and he watched her as she put her arm through the crook of Maxine's arm. Leaning over, she whispered something into Maxine's ear, her breast rubbing gently against the woman's sleeve.

Ralph ground his teeth in anger and turned away. He said to no one in particular, "What the hell time is it?"

Judy, her arms filled with fishing tackle and empty rum bottles, stopped in mid-stride and beckoned him with a jerk of her head.

"Here," she said. "Bend over and look at my watch."

Ralph turned her wrist toward him and peered through the darkness at the luminous dial. It said one-thirty. He scowled and looked at the sky. From the way he felt, he had figured it closer to four or five in the morning, time for daybreak, but the only light came from the looming edge of the city as they pulled closer to the shore.

Noah skillfully maneuvered the *Jim Boy* into a snug-fitting space along the pier. Two young men in snappily correct uniforms ran forward to tie the boat and help the women ashore.

Ralph walked slowly behind them down the runway, hardly noticing the cabin cruisers and sloops moored one next to the other for a mile along the beach. He felt a nudge at his back and turned to see Noah beside him, leading the dog on a chain. "You go with the lady," he said to Ralph, and nodded toward Maxine, walking ahead of them.

Ralph was about to refuse, but Alison, who had stopped to take Mars, smiled in agreement. "He's right," she said. "Maxine shouldn't go ahead unescorted."

Without a word to either of them, Ralph swallowed his anger and pushed ahead down the gangway until he caught up with the woman. His eyes narrow with hatred, he offered her his arm.

Maxine examined his creased clothes, then turned her head away contemptuously, her disdain even greater than his. "I'll see to it tomorrow that you are taken for a new wardrobe," she said. "Meanwhile, kindly keep away from me." She hurried her pace, and he was glad to let her escape him.

At the highway's edge, a black Cadillac limousine was waiting for them. The chauffeur, a plump man with red cheeks and livery to match, touched his cap deferentially to Maxine. Noah held the back door open while the women climbed in and settled themselves. Then he motioned Ralph to the front seat. Noah closed both doors and watched the limousine pull out into traffic.

They sped along the flat black asphalt, the heavy car smoothly picking up speed. They passed pink restaurants and green night clubs and rainbow-hued drive-ins lining both sides of the road. After a very few minutes, they came to a sign marking the Punta Verde city limits. The driver slowed the car.

Terraced hotels framed in curving palms and lush with the luxurious drapery of emerald-green elephant ears lined the road. Ralph tried to recall from whom he had heard of Punta Verde. Then he remembered that once a young writer had wanted to collaborate with him on an article about the wealthy "mainland" resort town. They had not been able to get the necessary legal permission, for Punta Verde was practically a closed town, an exclusive tropical paradise for the idle rich, and the idea had been dropped.

The chauffeur pulled into the pebbled drive in front of a hotel built of the local reddish sandstone, left rough-hewn and untinted to contrast with the shining black metal fishing rod curved in a thirty-foot arc by the pull of a blue neon marlin and mounted above the entrance. Between the rod and the fish, riding at a jaunty angle on blue neon waves, large letters spelled out: The Sportsman.

The chauffeur went around the car and opened the rear door. Ralph climbed out and contemplated the sports cars and opulent limousines fanned out around the entrance.

"This dump belongs to me," Judy said from close beside him, "so relax."

An inn-keeper, too, thought Ralph. Judy was full of surprises.

He turned to follow her into the lobby. The lobby of the hotel was decorated in a turquoise that deepened into blue, simulating the ocean's colors and making a flattering background for the suntanned couples who sat about idly talking or playing bridge. Ralph noticed that his companions were accorded little attention as they entered and climbed the spiral stairs.

"I suppose you'd like to get some sleep," Judy said as she took his arm.

Ralph looked down at her and smiled. He liked Judy and he felt almost comfortable with her. In her sweatshirt and yellowed sneakers, she looked as if she might be Huck Finn's kid sister. Certainly she did not appear a woman of twisted appetites, once a doctor, who happened to own a prosperous luxury hotel.

"Could use some sleep," he said simply.

Since they had entered the hotel, his head had begun a steady throb and now the line of his thoughts broke and darted off in a dozen different directions. Part of him relaxed and let the thoughts slide. Peggy … Ed … Maxine … Alison … seemed to merge in his mind.

Someone said, "But surely he isn't going to sleep so soon? It's still early. I wanted to go to the Town Bar." It sounded like Susie, but the voice seemed so remote that he could not be sure.

"You don't need him to go there." This voice came from right beside him, so it must be Judy's.

"I didn't say we needed him but what have we got him along for if we don't use him?"

"Well, you can see that he's practically dead on his feet." Alison's voice he would always know. "Why don't you wait until tomorrow?"

"No, my dear," said Maxine in the cold, level voice of authority. "Susie is quite right. As long as he is going to be with us, he might just as well do something. Judy can give him one of those pep pills or whatever you call the blamed things."

"Sure I can," Judy said, "but it would be a crime, after what this guy's been through. The human body can take a lot, but enough is enough."

"My dear friend," Maxine said quietly as she opened the door to an enormous office, "your caution comes a little late in life, don't you think?"

Judy smiled to herself and went around the huge desk to open the bottom drawer. "I suppose we could all use a little pep," she said. She took out a small amber-colored bottle.

Lillian, who had already settled herself into a prone position on a divan in the corner, lifted her chin and said, "Take pills without water? Darling, please!"

But Judy had anticipated her. From a cabinet built flush with the wall, she removed a bottle of gin and some glasses. "Won't this do?"

Ralph started to protest but watching Susie and Lillian and Alison herself each take a glass and one of the tiny pills, he decided to follow their example and wash down the tiny pill with a gulp of burning gin.

Only Maxine refused, having briefly shaken her head in answer to the question in Judy's eyes.

Still holding the empty glass in one hand, he sat down in a shell-shaped chair and stared across the room at the involved lines of a Picasso reproduction hanging on the wall behind Judy's desk. He could not tell how much time passed. The room, which had been dimly lit, suddenly glared in bright light and in a flash he realized that he comprehended the painting. He knew that his heart was beating rapidly and he felt vigorously alive with a newborn zest surging through his system. And what was even more important, he felt wildly, almost uncontrollably happy.

The others too began to lose their weariness. Lillian hopped off the divan and patted Judy fondly on both cheeks.

"Do we go?" asked Susie. "I'll race you all to the front door." She swung her arm for emphasis and a lamp teetered precariously.

Maxine's voice cut across her exuberance. "None of you is going out," she said flatly. "You'll all be either in jail or dead.

"I meant that only Ralph should take one of those pills, not the rest of you. That was unwise; the way you'll cut up now, you'll be in serious trouble or worse by morning."

Alison went to her, kissed her lingeringly on the throat. "If we're dead, then so much the better for us. And if we're in jail, you'll come get us, honey."

Maxine flushed deeply and twisted herself away from the girl's lips. "Don't be ridiculous," she said sternly. "You'll go nowhere all doped up like ... like juvenile delinquents. I've never seen such behavior in all my life. What's happening to you?"

Alison sighed and trailed her hand down over the woman's breast. "I'm just breaking out of my traces, darling. Don't you think it's time? I'm a big girl, now."

Maxine arose from her chair and stepped back out of the girl's reach. The skin across her cheeks was drawn taut. She struggled to find words but no sound came from her lips.

"Nothing's going to happen, Max," Judy said soothingly. "You know we've got this town sewed up tight. Why don't you calm down a little bit and come have yourself a ball with the rest of us?"

"When I want to have a ... a ball, as you call it, you won't have to ask me. We came to this place on business, not to make a scene. If any of you had any sense, you'd go off to bed this minute so you would be in decent shape for the conference tomorrow afternoon. Remember, the mayor and other officials will be there. We should be well prepared. Do you think I'm going to do all the work so the rest of you can sleep all day and run around all night? I am not a slave and I won't be treated like one. And I am not your conscience either. If you're going to behave like children, then you can just take care of this business by yourselves, without me."

"Don't let her go," Susie warned Alison.

Alison caught Maxine before she reached the door. She put her hand on the woman's arm. "Max, you're always right," she said slowly. "We're sorry." She turned to face the others. "Aren't we?"

Soberly, they nodded.

"We're sorry," echoed Lillian, as she flopped back on the divan.

Maxine shrugged off the girl's hand. "Then you'll all go to sleep," she said. "Right now." She stood at the door with her hand on the knob.

Alison pressed close to her and put her arms around her neck. Ralph, both fascinated and repelled, watched the feminine wiles come into play. It was, to him, a horrible and disgusting parody of a mischievous girl coaxing a recalcitrant male.

"But how can we go to sleep," Alison murmured against Maxine's ear, "if we're not sleepy?" She began stroking the woman's cheek with her fingertips and pecking her lightly on the lips. "Do you want us to fidget in bed all night long and get grumpy and miserable? How would we look coming into the meeting room all creased in the face and ugly? As long as we're awake, don't you think we might just as well have a little fun? It'll all be the same tomorrow. And besides," she rubbed the tip of her nose against Maxine's, "you didn't stop us from taking the stuff."

Defeated, Maxine sighed and disengaged the girl's arms from around her neck. She stepped back and smiled ruefully. "I can't fight you. I never could. But I told you—I didn't expect the rest of you to swallow that poison. I meant it only for him."

"You'll come along with us, won't you?"

"No. One of us has to be in good condition tomorrow. Basil is a reliable chauffeur. He'll see that you get there and back safely. And if you want to make public spectacles of yourselves, there's very little I can do to prevent it." She turned the knob and the door opened. "I'll be using Judy's bedroom," she said, looking at Alison significantly. "And please, all of you, try to conduct yourselves decently."

As the door closed after her, Ralph felt a sudden surge of elation and release. He felt a freedom he had not known for a long time. He grabbed Judy and swung her off the ground and around in the air.

"Hey, hang on!" she screeched at him. But he turned around and around with her until he crashed into the arm of a chair. They both fell dizzily to the floor.

The group stumbled down the hall, the stairs and out into the night. The chauffeur, Basil, was nowhere to be found. Lillian went to the Cadillac and peered into the window. "He didn't even leave the key," she said.

"Well, how about those others?" Susie waggled her fingers at a couple of sports roadsters.

"I guess we can borrow one of these." Judy pointed out a black Austin drop-head and a Jowett Jupiter with red leather seats. "They shouldn't mind. I've done enough for them." Her voice trailed off as she motioned the girls into the Jupiter.

Alison held back. "Too crowded," she said petulantly. "I want to drive the little Jupiter."

Judy sighed but did not protest. She went back into the lobby and returned dangling two sets of keys from her fingers. She handed one to Alison. "Okay, kid," she said. "You go first. We'll follow."

Alison took Ralph by the wrist and ran across the parking area, pulling him after her to the car. She opened the door and slid across the seat, a childlike grin lighting her face. Ralph got in beside her and watched her insert the key. He knew she had no idea of how little control she had over her movements but he felt strangely safe. Nothing in the world could go wrong. His guardian angel was smiling on him.

They swung in a wide, easy U-turn out to the highway and Alison slammed her foot down on the gas pedal. They zigzagged through early morning traffic. She kept her eyes straight ahead, concentrating on the road.

Now and then a horn behind them would warn that they were going much too fast for the dumpy little Austin to keep up with them. Alison would laugh with delight, slow down for just a moment, then press her foot hard on the pedal once more. Ralph watched her face, its every expression, the lips as they pursed in annoyance or relaxed in a smile. She had chosen him to ride with her. He refused to believe that she felt she had to play watchdog with him. Could it be that she honestly wanted to be with him but scarcely dared admit it to herself? He pondered the question, wondering when the time would be ripe to force the issue.

Twenty minutes later they pulled up in front of a small bar with an olive green curtain on a brass pole stretched across the window. The Town Bar's weatherbeaten sign was barely twelve inches high and placed low over the door. Ralph heard the faint sound of bongo drums inside.

He followed Alison to the entrance, where they waited for Judy and the others. They went into a long, crowded room, the air hanging heavy with cigarette smoke and the odor of stale beer.

The group was led to a round table, one of the two dozen that lined the dance floor. In the center of the floor, a green light muddying the pigment of their skins, three Negroes squatted on their toes with red-striped bongoes clasped between their knees. A fourth, sitting cross-legged on the floor in front of them, wailed shrilly on a reed-like instrument, his eyes closed, his body swaying like a charmed snake. As the tempo increased, a low grunt suddenly cut off the beating. In dead silence a barefooted Negress padded out into the spotlight. She stood still for an instant, then raised her arms and began rattling small gourds of seeds held in her palms. As her wrists rose, the beating of the drums was resumed. The tempo grew faster. Her heels thudded against the floor, calves and thighs flexed, ribs heaving and breasts hanging naked. Her stark white eyeballs rolled upward as her frenzy mounted.

Only when the dancer had finished and the musicians had retired from the floor did the waiter come forward to take their order. Judy, knowing what would mix with the stimulants already in their systems, ordered for all of them. A tenor uke, trap drum and piano combo began playing easy dance music. Ralph was mildly surprised to see that men and women started dancing together. He had begun to take for granted that the mixing of the sexes belonged to another world, another heritage.

He stood up and moved Alison out to the dance floor. She did not protest. He put his arms around her firmly, his fist gently pressing her close against him, his feet stepping into a fox trot. They glided off among the other couples.

The band moved easily from one tune to another without taking a break. Alison's body gradually molded itself to his. He felt her cheek lightly touch the side of his jaw and she responded to him with pleasure. Whatever hostility she had felt was gone.

The tiny dance floor became crowded and their steps grew smaller. Soon they were scarcely dancing at all, merely swaying together in time to the music, moving a step now and then when an opening appeared. He held her tightly to him and she surrendered herself to the pressure of his arms, letting him do with her as he pleased.

He was baffled. Sometimes she seemed to detest him—at other times she seemed to want him, openly and sincerely. Suddenly he realized that she was probably just as confused as he was ... if not more so.

When the music ended, Ralph took her by the hand and led her back to the table. At his place stood a cocoanut shell with two pink straws in it.

"It's about time," commented Lillian.

Alison did not reply. She put her lips to her drink and for a moment closed her eyes. Ralph watched her closely. He had a sudden impulse to touch her under the table with his knee, but he laughed to himself at the stupidity of such a move. She would find it incredibly naive. He couldn't take his eyes from her.

When the band returned to the stand, Susie leaned over to Lillian and said with a pout, "You haven't asked me to dance."

"True." Lillian lifted an eyebrow. "Shall we tell the world, darling?"

"What do you care if everybody wants to act straight tonight? If you really loved me, you'd ask me to dance." Her voice tightened with anger and petulance. She was well on the way to being drunk.

Lillian put a hand on the girl's arm and stroked it soothingly. "Anything you want, angel." She stood up and began pushing her way past tables toward the dance floor, taking Susie with her.

Judy leaned back and sipped at her drink. "That girl's a dancing fool, she is." Her genial eyes followed the pair out to the floor.

The two danced well together, Ralph noticed. Taller than most of the other couples, they were clearly visible. As though their move was a signal for the party to begin, other women moved out to the dance floor in couples, leaving the men to converse among themselves. Six pairs of women, exquisitely gowned in cocktail dresses and glittering with jewelry shared the floor. Then a tall, handsome boy with strawberry blond hair led another boy out to dance. What had a few minutes previously been a normal-looking barroom was turned into the misty twisted world Ralph thought he had momentarily escaped. He sighed and leaned back in the chair, his high spirits beginning to fade.

Alison too had been watching the change. She leaned forward eagerly and her eyes were amused. She asked Judy to get her another drink and Judy called the waiter.

"What you need, old girl," said Alison, speaking with her lips around a straw, "is a nice, patient little thing who'll teach you how to move around the dance floor in time to that drummer."

Judy laughed with real amusement. "I can make out all right on the dance floor," she said. "The question is, with whom?"

"Are you saying there isn't a gal in this place who could inspire you?"

Judy lit Alison's cigarette, then offered the light to Ralph. "With the exception of one."

"Seriously?"

"Seriously."

Alison took a deep breath and looked around. "Well, let's see what we can find. ..."

Ralph leaned forward and put his elbows on the table. This kind of hunt should be interesting. He spotted a slim brunette, with a boy's haircut, sitting between two men at a table and laughing easily.

"How about that one?" he asked, nodding in the direction of the girl.

"Phooey," said Alison. "She's straight."

Ralph shrugged. 'Well, how the devil am I supposed to know?"

"You're not," Judy replied. "This kind of thing takes an intuition that comes only from years of experience."

He was about to answer when he realized that Judy had suddenly lost interest in him. He turned to follow the line of her vision and found himself staring at the back of a woman in a low-cut gown. She was leaning on her palm, talking to a blond boy who was lighting one cigarette from the stub of another.

"Found it?" asked Alison.

"Maybe," muttered Judy. Abruptly she stood up, pushed back her chair and started across the room, shouldering her way past couples who stopped dancing to look at her. She was oblivious to everyone but the brown-haired woman with the graceful back.

Ralph and Alison watched her. She reached the table and stood there quietly for a minute, The woman turned her head and looked up at her. She smiled and put out her hand to take Judy's, motioning for the boy to get another chair.

"No fair," said Alison. "She knows her."

Ralph wondered if Alison realized that she was sitting alone with him at the table. She gave no indication that she did. She sipped her drink without looking at him once.

"Want to dance?" he asked.

She shook her head. "Not now," she said. "It's too crowded. I like lots of room, like there was when we first danced. Then I could dance all night." She laughed, her head flung back, her hair swinging.

"Maybe you need a change." He watched her stir the straw in the empty shell. "Want to walk around outside for a while?"

"Say, that's a good idea, but we have to remember to come back."

"We will."

She took a twenty-dollar bill from her pocket and let it flutter carelessly to the table.

"So the waiter won't think we're skipping," she said. "You have to be careful about waiters, especially in a queer place." She waved vaguely in the direction of the women on the dance floor as Ralph led her out past the crowded bar.

The air outdoors was warmer than it had been inside. Ralph felt a little of his good spirits return. He picked up Alison's hand and looked at the small, diamond-trimmed watch on her wrist. It was three-fifteen. A few stragglers were still on the sidewalks and he listened to their footsteps echoing loudly against the concrete.

Alison impulsively put her arm through his. "Know something?" she asked, watching their feet as they strolled.

"What?"

"You could be my cousin without half trying. There's something about you that's just like my cousin." She turned to smile up at him, mischief in her eyes. He wondered what she meant by it.

He put his hand on her shoulder and kept her from veering off the curb. "Which cousin?"

"Oh, any cousin," she said in an offhand way. "Wouldn't you like to be my cousin?"

"I certainly would. Shall we start right now?"

She stopped and looked up at him. "Right now," she said. She held out her hand and they shook solemnly. "Hello, cousin. Welcome to the clan."

"Hello, cousin, yourself," he said. "Now that we're related, I want you to tell me something."

"All right."

"The truth, now."

She lifted her hand and assumed a deadpan expression. "So help me."

"I want to know how much money we're going to inherit when we come of age."

Alison's shoulders drooped and she turned away from him. "Don't make me think about that," she said.

"Well, as a member of the family, I was just curious. Have to protect my interests, you know."

"Oh, what's the use of thinking about the past? Max says we're going to make it all back with the resort project. She's positive of it and it sounds pretty good to me." She took his hand as they walked. He nearly groaned aloud at her touch. "I never knew my parents, really. They died when I was too young. Maxine raised me—and she spent my money. So what?"

"All right," he said. "I thought it must be something like that." He increased their pace. "You can stop looking so mournful. She's got a real good idea in the works and the bank account's going to bloom. There's no reason why you can't relax and enjoy yourself without worrying about her, is there?"

There was a long pause. Alison looked trapped. "I suppose," she said finally. "But it's so hard to look her straight in the face unless I'm one hundred per cent on her side. You don't understand this, but there aren't any halfway paths with Max. There never are with people like her. Their pride is so sensitive that unless you're all the way with them, they think you're against them."

"Doesn't that ever put you in a dilemma? I mean—"

They had made their way, without realizing it, to the center of town. They passed by a small park. Alison brushed her fingertips across the tops of the benches as she walked, and he knew from the straight, stubborn line of her back that she was not going to answer.

Ralph had sensed in the first moment he had met Maxine that she was humbling her pride. She certainly was not the type of person to cater willingly to the whims of people who sought lavish, off-beat entertainment. Rather, he suspected, she would try to hide any connection with that sort of thing behind the veil of conventionality. He knew by her aloof attitude that she did not associate with these women by choice, that she actually detested them and deplored their lack of discretion. Now the mystery was solved. His question to Alison about money had been purely a stab in the dark but it had paid off.

His next step was to convince Alison that her pity was misplaced—for he believed that it was only pity that bound her to Maxine.

A few blocks beyond the park he heard the thud of rolling surf in the distance and he directed their footsteps toward the shore.

"I'll tell you the truth," Alison said as they stood looking down at the beach.

"Tell me."

"Judy could be a lot happier if she had a little more confidence in herself. She thinks she's too fat."

Ralph could not have cared less about Judy at the moment, but he listened attentively, knowing that Alison was enjoying the sharing of trivial intimacies with him. He suspected that she had no friends except the weird women with whom she traveled.

"And because of that, she lets the rest of herself go, too. I told her once that if she would only comb her hair and put on a little make-up...." She was following him down a steep path to the sand, picking her way carefully over the stones and jagged rocks.

"I think she's attractive," Ralph said. "She has a friendly kind of good looks. It probably appeals to more people than she realizes."

They stood on the damp sand, looking out at the ocean and breathing heavily after the exertion of their descent. The water rolled in on tiny waves, catching the moonlight and spreading it across the beach.

"Anyway," Alison continued, "that woman, whoever she was, seemed glad to see her."

Ralph stooped and sifted grains of sand through his fingers. "I think we can sit here. Not too damp."

She dropped down and leaned back on the palms of her hands. "This is wonderful," she sighed, drawing the sea air deep into her lungs and holding it there, her head pulled back, her eyes closed.

Ralph, squatting beside her, wished the moment would never end so that he could gaze forever upon the beautiful young face he treasured.

"Ocean lovers," she rambled on, speaking as much to herself as to him, "are a different species. Ever try to get an ocean lover to live in New Mexico? He kind of rolls up like an autumn leaf and crackles into little pieces."

"Well, bless the Lord, you have good sinuses."

She looked at him and smiled. "I have fine sinuses," she said, "and I bless the man who invented skin diving. Do you like to spear fish?" She leaned over to take off her sandals.

"I've done it a little," he said. "Most of the shooting I do is with the camera but maybe one of these day we can get together."

She slipped one sandal into the other and flipped them away from her onto the sand. "There'll be plenty of time in a couple of weeks," she said. "When they start bringing the building materials over to the island, we can probably find an excuse to go diving every day."

"Say, fine. Then I can finish that damned assignment that's hanging over my head."

She looked at him questioningly.

"I was supposed to be working on a photo series when I met you," he explained. "Kept holding off for a barracuda or something like it. Then you came along and … well, the poor guy's still waiting for the pictures."

She twisted around, put her head in his lap and looked up into his eyes. "You want to go hunting barracuda? Are you looking for trouble?" He was pleased to hear a slight note of concern.

Stroking her hair, he said, "Chances are he'll never know I'm there. They often swim right by a tasty morsel." He cupped her face in his hands. "Don't tell me you're worried?"

"Of course I'm not worried," she said. "It's just something that I've never done myself."

"Then you should be looking forward to it."

"Oh, I am. I am."

They sat close together in contented silence. Ralph wondered if she would feel as companionable toward him in the morning, when the drug had worn off. Even if she would not, he felt that he understood her better than ever before and that he was not far from finding the key that would, once and for all time, free her of Maxine's bonds.

The moon disappeared, yet the two figures remained, wrapped in a mutual peace. Ralph thought of the nights they had shared on the island and he realized that this was an evening infinitely richer. He had known nothing of her then but the beauty of her physical self and, at the time, nothing else had mattered. But now he knew something of the spirit that warmed the body.

Alison lay with her eyes closed, her breathing deep and even. She was asleep. Carefully he unbuttoned his shirt and spread it on the sand. He lifted her gently from his lap and laid her head on the cloth. She stirred a little to find a more comfortable position and then she slept peacefully again.

Ralph smoked his last cigarette. He felt a deep, inner elation. He knew that Maxine would never believe that he and Alison had slept innocently beside each other on the beach—nor could

Maxine ever know the power of such shared innocence. It could exist only between a man and a woman, deliciously tantalizing the wellsprings of ultimate passion.

Alison stirred and Ralph smiled down at her. He took her hand in his, kissed it and then put his head next to hers on the shirt. They both slept.

CHAPTER SEVEN

A FIRM GRASP on his shoulder shook Ralph out of a deep sleep. He rolled over and blinked up into the face of a coffee-colored native policeman. The eyes regarded Ralph questioningly, demanding an explanation.

Ralph scowled in annoyance. To his surprise, the response in the policeman's face was one of apology.

Ralph said, "All right now, beat it."

The cop hesitated.

"I said, get the hell out of here if you want to keep your job. Don't you know who I am?"

"But...." Seeing Ralph stare fixedly at his badge number, he changed his mind about saying anything and beat a hasty retreat from the beach to the street.

Ralph smiled. He would have been surprised had the man refused to be bullied. Just how corrupt the civic organization was, he did not care to think, but it was probably the safest city in the world for a rich man to commit murder.

He turned to look at Alison and saw that she was still sleeping heavily. The morning sun had brought a delicate sheen of perspiration across her forehead and the dampness had curled her fine hair into tiny ringlets over her ears. A pity, he thought, to awaken her.

He stood up to stretch his legs, turning to look back at the town and then out across the water where white sails already bellied in the breeze. He heard the girl stir beside him, becoming restless in the warm sunlight. He bent over and touched her shoulder.

She opened her eyes, stared at him blankly, trying to remember the circumstances that had brought them together there on the beach.

"I must have been pretty drunk," she said sleepily. "How much did I talk?"

"Not so much."

She sat up. He retrieved his shirt, shook the sand out of it, put it on and rolled up the sleeves to the elbows, meanwhile watching her closely. Was she friend or foe this morning?

"Well, they're probably frantic," she said anxiously. "Let's catch a cab." She was on her feet and looking around for her sandals.

Ralph tossed them to her and sat down to put on his own shoes. "Wouldn't you like to stop somewhere for coffee first?"

He saw her waver for a second, but she shook her head. "I'm not even sure it would go down," she said. "Besides, there'll be plenty of coffee at the motel."

He looked at her. She seemed upset, almost afraid, and once more he felt Maxine reach out to come between them. In silence, Ralph followed as Alison started up the path toward the street. She stood at the curb, peering up and down for a cab.

"Why don't you phone?" he offered. "It'll relieve your mind and you won't have to rush so."

"Yes, that's a good idea."

They turned up the street toward the little park and the line of stores beyond. The women who passed by were in bathing suits and many of them were accompanied by children carrying sand pails and water toys. A few fathers were also in evidence. Ralph found it strange to see families. He had thought of the resort as the kind of place reserved for people who would not tolerate youngsters, let alone produce them.

He glanced at Alison to see if she shared his wonder. Apparently she did not. She was looking intently for a place from which to phone.

They found a red booth on the next corner. She went inside and closed the door. When she came out, her anxiety was gone and the old ease was in its place.

"Everything all right?"

A slight nod of her head was her answer. "But we haven't much time." She glanced quickly at her watch. "It's almost noon. We have to eat, pick you up a respectable suit of clothes and get back to the motel before three. Maxine told me she's already had to postpone the meeting till four-thirty as it is." He watched as a minute of sadness clouded her face. Then it was gone and she smiled. "Come on," she said, "if we're going."

They found a comfortable corner in a leather-walled restaurant and ordered scrambled eggs and a pot of coffee. The food made them both feel better and they chatted amiably. Alison pulled her last five-dollar bill from a pocket and left the change for a tip. They walked back into the morning glare.

"Say, how are we going to get me a whole new outfit when we're both broke?" he asked.

She took his arm and they ran across the street, cutting through the traffic.

"Don't be so nosy."

She led him into a rather small but obviously expensive men's store featuring, in its window, linen and silk shantung suits with green velvet scarves at the throats. Ralph had a vision of himself being rigged out like a complete sissy.

A thin little man, immaculately dressed in one of the silk suits, emerged sedately from behind the counter where he had just put away a bolt of material.

He bowed slightly. "Good day," he said in a high, shrill voice. "May I help you?"

"I hope so," Alison said. "I'd like a dark gray suit for him. Single-breasted, please. And we need it right away."

The man nodded. "Won't you be seated?"

"Thank you." Smiling, she chose a blue leather chair beside a three-way mirror. Ralph thought about her taste and wondered how she would furnish a home.

The man disappeared behind a blue curtain and returned carrying three suits on heavy mahogany hangers. He lifted them to a rack. Before he had a chance to say anything, Alison stood up and flipped through them.

"Try this," she said, holding one out toward Ralph.

Obediently Ralph went into a spacious dressing room and put on the suit. He buttoned the jacket over the creased and tieless shirt, then returned for her inspection.

He watched her eyes move slowly from the trousers upward. He knew, with pride, how flat his stomach lay, how slim was the line of his hips, how wide were his shoulders. He knew, too, by the pinkness of her cheeks that her eyes did not appraise the suit alone. He was pleased that she was aware of the body beneath the clothing.

"I like it." She turned back to the salesman. "Now you can tell me where the nearest place will be for shirts and shoes."

"Yes, madam. That will be on Lane Street, just around the corner."

While he measured the suit for alterations and cuffs, Alison took a business card from the counter and hastily scrawled across the back of it. She handed the card to the clerk, who read it and nodded deferentially. She started out the door, Ralph following her.

"What in hell did you give him in there?" he asked, hurrying after her down the street. "The answer to next week's crosswords?"

She laughed. "Nope. A year's subscription to the *Reader's Digest*."

He took her arm. "I'm jealous."

"Don't be. He's even going to clean and press your old suit and have it sent home."

"Yeah? Where's that?"

The flip remark misfired and he felt her body tense. They could kid and joke but he was never allowed to forget that their moments together were stolen. For reasons he did not fully understand, she continued to wear Maxine's tether. Well, he'd be damned if he would wear it with her. Didn't she know that she didn't have to, that pity for Maxine did not have to mean submission to her? Some day Alison would know what real submission was, with no reservations.

They found the shirt shop, a narrow little store wedged between a native flower-stall and a Chinese restaurant. A lightweight white on white was her choice, which was fine with him, but he fought and won out against French cuffs. She picked a rose-checked tie that he was dubious about but it was by far the best tie in the store, so he allowed it. Besides, it would look all right with the suit.

A pair of black, plain-faced oxfords, purchased three or four doors down, finished the job of clothing Ralph. In the cab riding back to Judy's motel, Alison sat at the far side, gazing silently out the window, her thoughts withdrawn. He could get nowhere with conversation. Finally he rolled down the window, lit a cigarette and began to consider the business ahead. Alison had told him enough for him to gather that he would be meeting the town's most prominent citizens. He wondered how much they would put up with from tourists to increase local revenue. They would probably even welcome a queer set-up like this. It would be a nasty kind of fun, watching the monkeys jump for the peanuts. No doubt Maxine was quite ready to pay any graft required.

He wondered if the whole crew of them would be going. Of what possible use could Susie be in such a gathering? If Maxine had any business sense whatsoever, she would know that the fewer, the better. He doubted that he dare suggest as much to her, especially after the past night.

He had expected Maxine to be waiting for them in the lobby. But as they entered the motel, he saw no familiar faces. They strode across the floor and up the stairs. On the second-floor landing they ran into Judy. Her chocolate-brown suit warmed her eyes to a deep amber.

"Welcome home," she said, her lipsticked mouth spreading into a welcoming grin. "Her majesty awaits your company. She's in my bedroom." She jerked a thumb toward a door at the far end of the corridor.

Alison said, "Thanks," and they walked rapidly down the hall.

Ralph turned the knob. The door swung open and they were face to face with Maxine. She sat in a high wicker chair, the back of it spreading out above her like a fan. She glanced at them both, then her eyes fixed on Alison. The woman held a swizzle stick which she had been tapping on the rim of a glass on the table beside her. The room, decorated in the same light wicker as the chair, was a bland yet flattering background for her forceful personality. She wore a violet dress with a high collar that accentuated the strong line of her jaw.

She ignored Ralph pointedly. The deliberateness of it, the blindness of it, brought a touch of pity to mix with his hatred. He watched her, sitting majestically on her throne, an old-world aristocrat displaying a stubborn facade to an unrelenting world. He had the feeling that somewhere behind the facade there was a tiny hole in an unseen vein causing her to bleed to death slowly.

Maxine motioned Alison to her with a slight tilting of her regal head. She seemed to somehow command all of her situations by the means of bodily movements, as though she were used to being surrounded by servants ready to obey her every wish.

The girl stepped forward. She seemed to have forgotten Ralph, or perhaps she was simply ignoring him because Maxine did. The woman stared intently into Alison's face, deep into her eyes, searching for something there.

When she had found it, she relaxed against the chair, permitting herself a smile, and patted the girl's hip. Alison lifted the woman's glass and took a sip from it. She made a wry face.

Maxine smiled. "You should have recognized it."

"I guess I couldn't take anything this morning, let alone a Tom Collins."

"Afternoon," Ralph corrected.

From their reaction, he might just as well have uttered a four-letter word. Maxine turned and glared at him. "You can wait for me in Judy's office," she said, in that special tone of loathing he knew she reserved for him alone.

Previously, when he had been afraid that Alison might slip away from him forever, Ralph had considered it wise to bow to Maxine's wishes. But now, feeling a new confidence as a result of the past twenty-four hours, he was worried no longer. He had no intention of jumping through hoops for Maxine any more. The woman was a pitiful bluff and he knew it.

Instead of leaving as she had commanded him to do, he sat down on the edge of the bed and took a cigarette from a pack lying open on the bedside table. The sound of the striking match seemed loud in the taut silence.

It took Maxine a full minute to realize his intentions. Her composure and her dignity remained intact but her voice lowered almost to a whisper.

"Mr. Thayer, I said you were to leave."

Ralph took a deep drag on his cigarette and expelled the smoke sharply through his nose. "I heard you," he said.

He leaned back against the headboard and swung one foot upon the pale green bedspread. Maxine glanced around the room. Looking for another fishing rod, Ralph thought to himself. Well, just let her try something like that again and Alison would see her beloved aunt crippled.

Alison put her hand on Maxine's arm, both to soothe her and let her know she sided with her against Ralph.

Ralph was sick at her sudden desertion. He should have expected it, he supposed. Looking at the two of them and seeing the challenge in both pairs of eyes, he was suddenly and acutely depressed. What the hell was the use, anyway? Nothing would be accomplished by sitting there in hostility. At the same time, it irked him to give Maxine the satisfaction of his leaving.

He remembered Alison in his arms. She had been eager. He had not imagined it. He looked closely at her face. Was there, maybe, a silent pleading beneath the ferocity? Yes, he was sure there was. Without hesitating further, he stood up and turned his back on them, walking angrily to the door.

Once outside, his mind started to run wild and he thought he would go mad, picturing what might be happening between the two women now that they were alone. With terrible vividness, he recalled the image of them naked together at the hotel.

There was no doubt in his mind that Maxine was even now preparing to possess the girl. *His* girl. It had been convenient for her to postpone the meeting so that she might have these moments of privacy with Alison. Or, it occurred to him, had it been Alison's doing? It was apparent that Alison submitted willingly. He had a sudden impulse to whirl around and bash down the door of the room. He wanted to do violence, to smash forever all the bonds between them. But even as he thought of it, he knew it was no good. Alison would resent being dragged away by force. Such methods would ruin his own position with her ... while strengthening Maxine's.

If he were going to win the girl away from her demon lover, he knew it would have to be by more subtle means than brute force. She must be allowed to make the choice herself.

And yet he could not just trot on down the hall to Judy's office and simply wait. He felt that he would go insane, imagining the things that were happening but not really knowing whether they were. If he could just see something, anything. If he could only know what he was fighting.

He decided to throw away all scruples. He meant to get a look at them—at any cost.

He started turning doorknobs.

At the third try, the door swung open at his touch. He stepped into a room where a man's bathing trunks and a woman's wet suit hung twisted on the arm of the reading chair. He heard someone singing in the shower. He crossed directly to the window and stepped out onto the terrace. It was a narrow walk of black stone facing on the ocean. Waist-high partitions of the same stone marked the rooms from the outside. He had only to step across these and go past the intervening windows to reach his destination.

By the time he arrived at the terrace outside their room, he was in a cold sweat and crossed his fingers momentarily for luck. He knew that wide drapes hung at both sides of the wall-length windows. He could easily stand there without being seen. The windows were open slightly and he edged forward silently, hardly daring to breathe.

Through the open window he heard the quiet sound of their voices. Low and intimate, they murmured together like zephyr and wavelet. The tones intermingled tenderly, lingeringly, their words touching like lips, their sighs caressing like moving fingers. A sharp intake of breath, a shudder of pleasure. Then relaxing again into the playful whisper.

Breathless now with rage, Ralph edged forward. The bed was diagonally opposite the window. Vaguely he could make out the blurred image of a figure, its tanned back bent, leaning over, rocking gently back and forth, its lips grazing the white neck and shoulders that lay beneath it. Ralph was amazed to see how young Maxine's physique appeared even next to the vigorous, healthy body of Alison. But in that one glance, he also realized that they were so engrossed in each other that they would not have noticed him had he been right there beside them. He grew bolder and peered closely into the room.

Alison had let her hair fall loose around her shoulders and Maxine's fingertips began to trace a line from the dark locks down the groove of her back. The girl shivered with delight.

Maxine moved suddenly and pulled the girl down tight on top of her, the flesh of their breasts pressing together. They clung ecstatically and Maxine whispered words into the girl's ear that did not reach Ralph.

Disgusted, yet hypnotically fascinated, he watched, dreading to see, yet not daring to leave.

Alison's tongue played with the woman's ear lobe and moved down to the hollow of her throat. Then, raising herself on her elbow, her hand caressed Maxine's breasts and suddenly she bent to kiss the darkened suffused tips. Maxine shuddered and arched her back. Alison stiffened. Their bodies surged wildly against each other ...

Ralph tore himself from the window and stared unseeingly at the ocean. Beads of perspiration ran down his face. The sound of Alison's pleasure filled his ears, the warm and sweet smell of her passion was in his nostrils.

Blinded by emotions of loss and grief, overwhelmed by a murderous rage, he rushed in a daze from the terrace and climbed through the first open window he came to. Three startled men turned from their pinochle game to watch him stride across the room and out to the hall.

He ran into Judy's office and locked the door behind him. He wanted to forget what he had seen. He wanted to erase it so completely that he would never recall it again. Maxine had been to him a creature to be pitied, one of life's misfits who had temporarily captured Alison through sheer accident. And just what was she now? Not pitiable, certainly. And certainly not someone to be lightly dismissed. She was a creature of power—a formidable enemy who could do anything he could do. Differently, perhaps, but maybe better. She was a person who knew more about Alison, more about pleasing her, more about teasing her, than he would be able to know for many a year.

No, Maxine was not a person to be pitied or scorned. He hated her for what she was, detested her twisted ways with Alison and despised her ruthless cruelty. But she was someone to be respected, an adversary who could be defeated only by exercising the greatest shrewdness. He couldn't afford to openly lash out against her.

He found Judy's liquor cabinet and poured himself a shot of bourbon, wondering if he really had a chance against Maxine after all.

He put down the glass, went to his own room, where he found his clothes had arrived. He swiftly showered, shaved, and donned the new outfit.

Then he returned to the office, and poured himself a second shot.

CHAPTER EIGHT

R ALPH HAD scarcely swallowed the drink when Maxine came in. Surprised, he stood up, waited for her to say something. She had on the same violet dress but she looked refreshed. Her hair was newly combed, her skin glowing pinkly as though from a hot shower.

"Pull yourself together," she said amiably. "We'll be leaving in just a few minutes." Her voice was friendly and her manner easy and comfortable. She even smiled a little.

Not trusting himself to answer, Ralph shrugged. His head felt warm and he wished there were snow on the ground—nice, crunchy snow—instead of the limp sand that surrounded the place.

"That suit becomes you," she said, apparently unaware of his hostile silence.

The more she said, the angrier he became. He did not want her to be nice to him. Not now, not after that. But after all, he thought, she could afford to be nice. The reins were in her hands again—or maybe they had always been.

"Yes, that's a good color for you," she said. "It lends strength, Mr. Thayer." She came around from behind the desk and looked through a bunch of papers she had taken from the left-hand drawer. She glanced up at him now and then with a casual comment. But her attention was drawn to what she was reading, and the one-sided conversation dwindled and then died altogether.

A few minutes later Judy entered. She sighed and put away the liquor bottle.

"Well, are we ready?" she asked.

"Yes. Have you a manila folder for these?"

Judy went to the desk and found a manila folder beneath the blotter. She held it open and Maxine dropped in the papers.

Without waiting for them to finish, Ralph went to the door and out into the hall. Followed by the muffled steps of the two women, he went down the stairs and outside. Basil was standing beside the car, his arms folded, his red face turned toward the slanting rays of the sun. He nodded to Ralph and opened the door for the two women. Judy motioned Ralph in beside her.

"Don't I sit up front?" he asked, getting in and settling into the corner.

"What for?" Judy replied. "There's room back here for the three of us."

"We're the only ones going?"

"That's right."

So the old bag did know how to operate things properly. No muss, fuss or clutter. Not even giving in to the temptation of having her thoughts diverted by the one person in the world who could do it. Basil pulled the limousine into the road and headed toward the outskirts of town.

Ralph was quietly amused to discover that the sweet odor coming to his nostrils was that of perfume. Judy had doused herself and sat there complacently giving off *eau de fleurs* like a pansy skunk. She and Maxine had a brief exchange of words about the contracts to be drawn up. They looked like a couple of school teachers dressed up for the class graduation.

The whiskey was beginning to settle itself in his stomach and he relaxed against the soft cushions, letting his head fall back and his eyes close. Basil drove with precision, never having to jam on the brakes, never taking a corner too fast. The hum of the motor, the low pitch of the voices, lulled Ralph to sleep.

He was dozing when the car slowed and the tires crunched on gravel. He blinked the sleep from his eyes and sat up straight.

They pulled up and parked in the driveway of a huge Georgian mansion. The great white building retired sedately behind a pair of Doric columns that framed the arched door. On the blue-green lawn stood two boys in their teens, intent upon teaching a frisky blonde cocker spaniel to beg. They waved hello to Judy and then paid no more attention to the limousine or its occupants.

A Negro butler opened the door and ushered them into a great hall. They followed him across a black-veined marble floor toward double ebony doors. Ralph noticed an ornate staircase leading to the upstairs floors. This, he knew, must be a government house. It was different from any he had seen in Punta Verde.

The butler pulled open the doors and stood aside as they entered a rose-colored living room just a few shades darker than Ralph's tie. Ralph wondered for a moment if Alison had been here before and had bought the harmonizing tie on purpose.

They seated themselves on velvet plush chairs and waited without speaking for a few moments. Then two men entered the room side by side with hearty, almost identical smiles and outstretched hands that reminded Ralph of candid photo shots in the newspapers on the eve of an election.

It was Judy who managed the introductions.

"Ralph Thayer, this is Harold Ross, governor of the territory and an old friend."

Ralph's hand was clasped in a firm grip while the man's other hand grasped his shoulder. He felt as if he were being pushed and pulled at the same time. The face before him had yellowed, nicotine-stained teeth and eyes sharp from lack of sleep. The dignitary's thinning brown hair was parted in the center. This was the kind of man who worked hard and made all those around him work equally hard. This was also a man with enough foresight to be a big fish in a little pool fattening himself on graft, rather than a sardine in a big ocean with all kinds of predators ready to fatten on him.

Behind him was a lean, smooth-faced young man, no more than twenty. His major resemblance to Harold Ross consisted of an artificial grin, which somehow spoiled an otherwise honest face. His features had a fineness that must have come from the mother and Ralph knew instinctively that the boy was not as friendly with his father as appearances might indicate.

Harold Ross put his hand back and brought the boy forward. "This is my son, William."

"Pleased to meet you, Mr. Thayer." The grin was still there but Ralph felt an undercurrent of shyness and uneasiness in the hand the boy thrust at him.

They were served whiskey and soda and for a few moments they chatted idly. Ross seemed to be in no hurry to get down to business. It was Maxine who finally broached the subject, lifting the envelope from her lap and holding it toward him.

"You'll find everything listed, I believe," she began without preliminaries. "Probable gross and net income, operating costs, transportation and so forth."

Mr. Ross extracted the sheaf of papers from the envelope, but he made no move to examine them. "That's all very fine," he said, "but how can you guarantee these figures as accurate?" He glanced for a moment at his son, as though trying to impress upon the boy the need for questions, the penetrating questions of an astute businessman.

"Come now, Mr. Ross," Maxine said. She folded her hands in her lap and she did not look very comfortable. "As a business-man, you are certainly aware of the fallacy in such a question."

"Of course, of course." He jiggled the ice in his glass and leaned forward on the edge of his chair. "But in a venture such as the one you have proposed, we can hardly afford to take chances." He cleared his throat. "I'm sure you all understand what would happen if this should result in a loss."

"Loss, Harold?" Judy's voice rumbled with deprecating laughter. "This certainly can't lose."

"Your optimism is warranted, Judy, I'm sure. But what can you give for security? This has nothing to do with me, I hope you understand. If it were only my say-so you needed. ..." He waved a hand grandiosely.

Maxine crossed her knees and reached for a cigarette in the carved box beside her drink on the low table. "I thought everyone was going to be here," she said. "Everyone with a say in the matter, that is."

"I am empowered to speak for them. But I'm sure you realize that there are many enterprises flourishing in this vicinity. Money flows in here as it does nowhere else in the world. You are fortunate that we were able to sell you the island, considering how many would have been glad to buy it. The mere act of filing the purchase stirred up enough curiosity to cost me a four-figure check."

"I'll reimburse you the first thing in the morning," Judy said, quick to take the hint. "In fact, I'll send you two checks just to keep the lovely peace. And I'd feel lots better if you could give me a paper or a deed that says we're entitled to the place. You know, a certificate of ownership, like when you buy a car."

Harold Ross laughed. "Anything you say. But I wish you realized the importance of assuring all the red-tape merchants that their yearly income from your venture will justify all the back-turning they're going to have to do."

Judy snorted and stood up. Her skirt creased untidily over her stomach and there were wrinkles in her jacket sleeves. She looked as if she was about ready to go fishing. "Okay. We'll straighten this thing out once and for all," she said. "This is the kind of deal I'll give you. If the resort doesn't pay the revenue stated on those papers, I'll personally make it up from my hotel's income. This will cover a period of five years, after which time, if it's obvious that the idea's a flop, we'll turn the whole thing over to the vultures to do with as their grimy little hearts desire. Fair enough?"

Maxine turned pale. "That's a deep hole you're digging, my friend." Her voice was low.

Judy smiled. "Not deep enough for a grave."

"You ladies must certainly be convinced," Ross said. "Don't you agree, Mr. Thayer?"

"Definitely," Ralph said automatically. He was watching Maxine and seeing the parade of horrors in her mind. What a blow to her pride, to have to put herself and her friend into this financial straitjacket. He knew she would stop at nothing, probably not even murder now, to assure the success of this venture. Her stern face set with determination as she watched Judy shake hands with the governor.

"If you will come down to my office tomorrow, any time at your convenience, Judy, we'll have the necessary papers drawn up."

"Fine."

Ross nodded for his son to refill the glasses. "As for the details of operation," he said, "I'm sure that we can safely leave them in the hands of the construction company. However, you assure me that there will be enough room for a boat to pass through the reef and into the lagoon without endangering any lives. Is that right?"

Maxine said, "You might ask Mr. Thayer. He has been to the island underwater."

"Is that so, Mr. Thayer?" asked the governor, a note of surprise in his voice.

"Yes." Ralph sighed. He did not feel like talking about the island, or about swimming through the reef. Those places belonged to another part of his life, a very personal part. Sitting there in the big room, he felt that maybe the ocean didn't even exist, that swimming silently through the sea was forever a thing of the past for him, never to be repeated. The memory of Alison lying naked on the sand, of their long days and nights together, crowded into his mind and silenced his tongue.

"Well, man," said Ross with enthusiasm, "tell us something about it."

"What is there to tell?"

"Come now," Maxine said sharply. "You don't want to appear modest."

She knew perfectly well that it wasn't modesty keeping his mouth closed. And he knew she wanted him to talk, to tell them everything, to share the wonders of the island so they would lose their precious, secret quality. He looked at her and smiled, letting her know he saw through her jealousy.

"Well, to be honest," he began, "the reef is by no means a simple thing to navigate. But the coral formations have many wide gaps in them and it shouldn't be difficult to blast a channel wide enough for a fair-sized boat. It would take such a craft no more than half an hour to make its way from the mainland, once a channel were cut out and dredged."

Governor Ross offered him a cigar and when Ralph declined, he peeled back the cellophane, bit off the end and unconsciously spat it across the room. "You, of course, will direct the blasting and later take over the navigation of the supply boat, Mr. Thayer?"

"If necessary."

"Certainly it will be necessary," the governor said firmly. "Putting all this in the hands of someone who has to grope his way out there might cause damage not only to the vessel but to lives as well. We can't afford to take a chance like that. I'm afraid you'll have to take on the job."

Ralph felt a grin tugging at the corners of his lips. "With pleasure," he said, politely inclining his head toward Maxine. He had not realized how valuable he could be to her.

His head was beginning to whirl. He had been taking aboard too much alcohol. William crossed the room to him, offering to fill his glass. Although he shouldn't have, Ralph accepted.

He wondered what Mrs. Ross would say if she came into the room and discovered the kind of company her husband kept. Some company. Two queers and a jack-in-the-box.

That was all he was. A puppet who popped up and down like a silly fool, depending on whoever lifted his lid. For Alison, it was worth playing puppet. But for that perverted hag Maxine? Hell!

Judy said, "We seem to have covered everything that's important to you, Harold. I think we'll have to be getting back to the hotel."

Ross stood up. "All right, my dear. Everything seems to be in order. With your signed guarantee, I see no reason why we can't go ahead and complete this endeavor. You'll drop by my office and settle the minor points." He bowed to Maxine. "A pleasure seeing you again, Miss Carpentier." Then he turned to Ralph and extended his hand. "Good luck, Mr. Thayer."

Ralph accepted the hand. Tactfully Ross took him to the door and helped him down the three steps to the car.

Basil closed the car doors solidly and Judy waved a last good-bye to the governor. The car circled around the driveway and headed back toward the hotel.

When they reached the lobby, they found Lillian and Susie were waiting for them. The minute she caught sight of Judy, Susie rushed forward, clapping her hands and jangling the heavy Mexican bracelets that ringed her thin arm to the elbow. "When do we start?" she squealed loudly. "Do we start right away?" "Quiet down," Lillian said with an embarrassed grimace. "Want the fire engines to come roaring?" She took Judy's arm and started with her up the stairs. Susie was close behind them. "I suppose it's all set?"

"Yes."

"Goody, goody," Susie cried. "Now I can start sending out postcards."

"Sure," Maxine said, "but date them next year." Her eyes were darting around as if in search for someone.

With sudden daring, Ralph put it into words for both of them. "Where's Alison?"

"Gee, I don't know," Susie said. "We haven't seen her since last night. Gosh, you mean to say she hasn't come back yet?"

"She's been back. For heaven's sakes, don't be such an ass!" Lillian turned and gave her a look calculated to stifle further comment.

Ralph persisted. "Then where is she?"

"Yes," Maxine said. "I should think she might like to know how it went today."

He was aware that Maxine's hostility toward him had lessened considerably. Her conquest of Alison earlier in the day and the governor's recognition of his value to the project combined to make her treat him with something akin to tolerance. Otherwise, he knew, he would have been banished to his room as punishment for his drunkenness.

At the moment, however, he cared little about anything she might do. He felt awful. There wasn't enough sleep to rest him, enough food to quiet the grinding of his stomach, enough black coffee to bring him around. And certainly not enough love to fill his need. He wished he could find a quiet spot where he could put his head down and sleep forever.

When they were seated in Judy's office, Maxine announced there would be no point to discussing what had happened at the governor's mansion, since all would only have to be repeated for Alison's benefit. If someone would take a quick look around, they would probably find the girl in her room taking a nap or perhaps she had gone down to the beach for a quick swim. She presented such a stubborn face that no one dared to argue with her.

Ralph put his hands in his pockets and spread out his legs. Then he looked at his feet, changed his mind, and crossed them at the ankles. The black socks looked very respectable, he thought. Much too respectable to fall asleep in. He would have to stay awake somehow until it got dark.

"I will be a gentleman," he mumbled in what was meant to be a firm tone, "and look for the lady."

Judy stared at him dubiously. "It's a good thought. But maybe I ought to go."

"No," he said much louder than he had intended. "I am going to look for her."

"You're not even able to sit up straight, Mr. Thayer," Maxine said.

"I'll do better than that," he said. "I'll stand up straight." He pushed himself out of the chair and climbed to his feet. "How's that?"

Judy dusted a speck from his lapel. "Two bits says you can't make it down the stairs."

He tweaked her nose slightly. "You're on. Come watch and see that I'm not cheating."

"All right."

Judy opened the door for him and they went toward the stairs. He had more control over his legs than he had thought. Going down the steps was simply a matter of keeping himself attached to the bannister. Judy watched him from the landing and when he reached the last step, he turned and smiled at her, still holding fast to the bannister, and waved a hand in triumph. She waved back.

As he turned toward the door, Ralph caught sight of himself in the mirror and knew that he still looked pretty dapper. He did not feel dapper, though. He did not feel much of anything except a numbness in his legs. He felt as if he were walking knee-deep in cotton. Maybe, with a little luck, he would collapse. Then he could stretch out and be comfortable in a nice clean hospital bed where someone would feed him from a spoon and then let him sleep.

Maybe she was in a hospital, it occurred to him. She must be every bit as tired as he was, if not as drunk. Maybe he should call the hospital and ask if a dark-haired girl with the most beautiful eyes in the world had been brought into the emergency ward. The idea seemed a sensible one and he looked around the lobby for a phone.

He found a booth and then discovered that he had no coin.

Oh, well, she wasn't the kind to be sick, anyway. Might as well relax and take his time about finding her. The first thing on the agenda was a large breath of fresh air.

He made his way around the side of the hotel and down to the shore. He squinted into the dying sunlight, looking across the beach for Alison. Why couldn't she be sitting under one of the palm trees, reading a copy of *The Saturday Evening Post* or something? Where the hell was she, anyway? He was getting tired of this. He plowed across the sand to the water's edge, but she was nowhere on the beach or in the wide, wide ocean. He decided he might just as well go back to the hotel.

When he reached the lawn, he took off his shoes and shook out the sand. He kneeled to put them back on. Bending his head down was precisely the wrong thing to do. The lawn spun dizzily and his eyes watered. One thing for sure, he promised himself—no more alcohol. Not ever.

He wandered around the hotel, feeling like a ghost lost in someone else's dream. Faces swam by him like little fish, but none had the right eyes or nose or mouth. He became exquisitely aware that there was no other Alison in the whole world. And maybe the Alison he had known didn't exist any more. Maybe she had run away. Or maybe she had just vanished. He began to know a terrible fear and the need to find her became suddenly urgent. Sobering up, his mind began to function normally again.

He made a mental list of all the places where she might be. These he proceeded to methodically investigate.

Simply enough, he found her in the room she shared with Maxine. A rap on the door brought her to it and she looked up at him questioningly.

It did not occur to him to speak to her. It was enough to see the beautiful face, the slim body sheathed in a cool white dress.

"Well, come in," she said. "You don't have to stand there like a delivery boy."

He went in and sat down. The hell with Maxine, he thought. The hell with all of them. Let them wait forever. He looked at the bed. It was smooth and inviting, as unruffled as if it had never been used. Stupidly he found himself wanting to say something about it but a remnant of good sense stilled his tongue. He waited until he felt it was safe for him to speak.

"That Harold Ross," he said at last, "drives a damned tough bargain."

Alison was putting finishing touches to her make-up. Holding the lipstick to her mouth and looking at herself critically in the mirror, she asked, "What do you mean?"

"You people didn't get away as free and clear as you wanted to."

He lit a cigarette, enjoying the strong taste of the island tobacco. Then he told her in detail what had happened. She did not seem to be particularly interested or even to be paying much attention. Except for an occasional comment, he would have thought that she was ignoring him.

It did not seem to worry her that Judy had signed herself up to the ears. First of all, she said, the place was sure to be a roaring success. She listed the people they knew whose patronage would guarantee expenses and assure the income necessary to cover the figures quoted to Harold Ross.

Ralph sat back and listened to her without interrupting. He watched the excitement grow within her. When she talked like this, she displayed the animation of a young puppy and he liked it.

She went on to point out that, in the second place, even if the venture should not be the success they expected it to be in the first year of operation, Judy had more than enough money.

She wouldn't be faced with ruin no matter what happened. And beyond that point, she concluded, there was just no sense in trying to calculate.

He thought for a minute about not telling her that Maxine and the others were waiting for them down the hall. He even considered staying a while with Alison and letting Maxine worry herself frantic.

But what, after all, was the use? It didn't really seem worth all the trouble it might cause. There was no reason Alison should have to suffer at the hands of Maxine because of him.

Besides, Alison had asked him to come in. She had listened to him and she had been happy to hear of his new role as navigator of the supply boat. It was just a crumb, of course. But that was all he wanted for a while. Crumbs. Just let them keep coming his way—long enough for him to figure out how to get the whole cake.

So he told Alison that Maxine and the others were waiting.

As they walked toward the door, he casually put his arm around her waist. She stopped as if he had struck her and stood absolutely motionless.

"What's the matter?" he asked. "Did I do something wrong?"

"Don't," she said.

"Don't what?"

"Don't touch me. Don't ever touch me again." Her face was white under its tan.

He stepped back. "All right, if that's the way you feel about it, I won't. But I won't pretend that I understand."

"I can't explain it to you. I can't even explain it to myself. It's just that I can't go two ways at the same time, I guess." She brushed her hand across her forehead.

He put his arms on her shoulders. "You don't have to go two ways at the same time," he said softly. "That's what I've been trying to get across to you. I've been hoping you'd go one way only— my way."

She pulled away. "I don't know. Sometimes I think one way, sometimes the exact opposite. Maybe I'm just a two-way person."

"No, you're not—and you never will be as long as I'm around!" He pulled her to him, crushing her body against his. "This is what you want, see? This is what you want, this is what you need and this is what you're going to get!" He held her, brutally caressing her, probing with his fingers, his lips. She writhed in anger and frustration.

"Damn you!" she hissed. "Damn you! Why don't you go away? I don't want you! I'll never want you!"

But with her very words, her body met his, matching desire with desire, and her restless hips pushed against him with flaming urgency.

"I don't want you!" she repeated between clenched teeth. "Go away!" and she pounded her fists on his back in a frenzy of anguish.

"All right," he said, stepping back deliberately, every nerve in his body on fire. I must be insane, he thought, completely gone. There was a shocked silence in the room as time seemed to screech to a sudden halt. "All right, Alison. But just remember this. When you do want me, I'll be there. But you'll have to want me. Me, you understand? Me, Ralph Thayer. You'll have to want not just your own pleasure, but me!"

The dismayed horror on her face was unbearable. He turned quickly and left the room. She would have to pull herself together as best she could and join the others. He knew she was aware that Maxine was expecting her and that the time was not yet ripe for her to openly defy the woman ... not yet.

Reaching his own room, he threw himself down on the bed, fully clothed. His body burned with a painful desire and he knew that in a moment he would have to get up and take a cold shower.

CHAPTER NINE

L IFE BEGAN to take on new activity for all of them. The women had been waiting for their plans to be okayed by the governor and once Judy signed the final papers, their daily purposelessness ceased. Locked in the office, Maxine and Judy engaged in countless telephone calls. Absorbed in dozens of details, Maxine had no time to be bothered about Ralph and what he might mean to Alison. Instead of shutting him out, she began to seek his advice about construction details and transportation. And it became apparent to him that his skill as a photographer would come in just as handy to Maxine as would his knowledge of the underwater route.

Letters, telegrams and phone calls filled the hours. When the day's work was done, Maxine and Alison had little desire to go out. Ralph found that by ten o'clock his company was usually that of Susie. Restless and bored during the daylight hours, she seemed to snap on like a neon sign when the sun went down.

When he would look around for Alison he would usually discover that she had already retired with Maxine to their room. He could hardly afford to appear annoyed by her and yet there was little he could do to conceal his irritation. He refused to believe that she had to go to bed so early. Maxine would not force her to keep so stringent a schedule. It irked him that Alison never once sought a few minutes to spend alone with him at the end of the day. It disturbed him to think of her as being enslaved to Maxine.

Then it occurred to him that maybe Alison was shunning him chiefly in order to avoid trouble, for she seemed strangely determined that Maxine's venture be a success, seemed to hold this goal more important than any other.

He had to admit that things were going along smoothly. It was no novelty for him to see the pair up, dressed and down for breakfast by nine. And by ten they would be retired to the big office for the business of the day. Judy was a big help, too. Between them, Judy and Maxine disposed of the myriad business details with efficiency and judgment.

There was little left for Lillian and Susie to do, which suited them perfectly. They spent their days adventuring and their nights carousing—and seemed the happier, if not the healthier, for it.

But Maxine always managed to keep Alison right beside her and busy with some trifle or another. The girl applied herself with as much energy and good will as if she alone had been commissioned to achieve the venture's success. She was so wholeheartedly dedicated to Maxine's project that although she and Ralph often spent the whole day together in the same room, conversation between them was rare.

His helplessness sapped his energies or, more likely, his inability to sleep. After Alison retired for the night, he would walk around the lobby, smoking cigarette after cigarette. After a while he would begin to feel caged and would go out into the dark night and take the Austin, to which Maxine had provided him with his own key. The roar of surf along the ocean road would make him all the more restless. The little car could not go fast enough to outdistance his thoughts, and the heaviness of despair would grow inside him. Then he would find a bar and sit in a dark corner, seeking the solace of alcohol. After he became blurred enough not to distinguish the sharp points of his pain, he would drive back to the motel, climb up the stairs to his room, and finally lose himself in sleep—only to wake an hour or two later, and spend the rest of the night tossing fitfully.

One morning he was casually informed that they had arranged for a helicopter to fly him to the island so that he could photograph the terrain. Unknown to Ralph, his equipment had been brought over from Kinderman. Along with this piece of information, he was handed the familiar leather bags. Stooping beside them, he ran his fingertips over the scratches and grooves in the worn leather, recalling in snatches the many incidents that had left them there. Had those days been good ones for him, he now wondered. He remembered them as being marvelous but he knew that such nostalgia was not to be trusted, for if they had been so fine, why had he been so anxious to seek out a new path, a path that would lead him to ... to where he was now, perhaps?

He snapped open the lock of one bag and looked down curiously at the array of cameras and lenses in their leather straps. He did not want to touch them lest he ruin the picture he had in his mind of the life he was striving for. He had found it was like that sometimes with a camera. He could be walking down the street and suddenly see something that moved his spirit. He would lift the camera to his eye and snap. He would rush home to the darkroom, work quickly, excitedly. But when he held the final print up to the light, the special quality that had made him respond had somehow washed down the drain with the chemicals and he was left holding a lifeless imitation of the scene which had inspired him.

And that was what he had been recently wondering about himself. Was he living here among the islands a real life with Alison or was it all just a picture life? Strangely, he thought of Peggy. It had been a long time since he had sent her that cable. Admittedly, Peggy had been a bore but he had never been able to challenge her sincerity. Had he too, perhaps, been a bore? She must be at home, waiting to hear from him. Why hadn't he written to her?

Without bothering to check the contents, he closed the bag and nodded briefly to Judy.

"It's all here," he said, "but I'll be needing a lot of film."

If he had hoped for a delay because of the film, he was disappointed. Three dozen rolls had been bought for his Leica, more than enough to take the few daylight shots of the island that would be needed.

Going back to Kinderman would mean the certainty of finding there a letter from Peggy; in consequence, he decided he had better have the helicopter fly him directly to the coral isle. He could avoid Montrose, and the hotel and mail that way, although not indefinitely. There was a thousand bucks from Ed waiting for him there.

Alison was on the telephone, making final arrangements for the helicopter. Ralph switched off his thoughts and let himself be absorbed by the sound of her words. Listening to that voice, he realized that it was luring him to his own destruction—and that he didn't care. Whatever he tried to do with the rest of his life, no matter what happened, he would have nothing worth living for—he would be beyond the sound of that voice.

The flight was arranged for the following Saturday morning at nine. Since the weather at this time of the year was always the same, plus or minus a few clouds, he knew that the flight would take place on time. Distracted by his dreams, listless about cleaning his equipment, he almost shook his head when Maxine asked him if he would need any assistance, but then nodded violently.

"Yes," he said, grasping at the unexpected opportunity. "Come to think of it, I will need someone to hang on to all this stuff when I climb up to shoot the other side of the barrier. It's pretty rough terrain."

Apparently Maxine did not stop to think about his possible motives because she gave her ready agreement. He could have whatever or whomever he needed. She had lost much of the constant wariness with which she had at first treated him. She herself had changed. Her jackets were no longer buttoned tight to her throat. Her pallid skin had been turned a subtle pink by the moments she had managed in the sun. Occasionally, when she spent the day indoors, she even wore slacks. There were times when he passed her door and heard her laughing heartily at a joke shared with Alison or Judy. She was remembering what it was to enjoy life and the days of her austerity were fast fading.

Ralph had been observing this subtle change in Maxine and waiting for a chance to take advantage of it. Alison gave her no trouble. She did whatever Maxine asked of her and her affection for the woman seemed so obvious that Maxine had lost much of her fear of Ralph. And, the project too, was going well. In fact, Maxine seemed to lack nothing that ambition and love could supply. Ralph watched her as a cat watches a butterfly, knowing she was off guard and anxious that she remain that way.

In the most casual tone he could muster, he said, "I'll need someone familiar with the layout. It's a tricky business, climbing around on that coral, you know. One good tumble and there goes all my work."

Maxine said it herself, not suspecting that she had fallen into a trap. "Well, in that case, I suppose you'd better take Alison."

Ralph nodded, his glee hidden behind a straight face. "I guess so," he said. He managed to sound almost reluctant.

No one thought twice about the situation and for this Ralph was thankful. In a new state of mind and with something definite to look forward to, he no longer found it necessary to go barflying. He sat in his room, smoking, vividly reliving the thrills of being alone with her.

The days of waiting were endless, he thought, and the nights more so but Friday evening arrived at last. He undressed and went peacefully to bed, enjoying the first really sound sleep he had had since meeting Alison.

He was up and dressed by dawn, pacing the floor of his room, anxious to be on his way. His sunburn had faded, he noticed, staring into his shaving mirror. But then, so had the black lines under his eyes. In fact, he felt that he looked rather well. He pulled himself up tall, patted his flat belly and went down the stairs with confidence.

Alison had dressed for the occasion in black twill trousers and red shirt. She came down the stairs to the lobby, tucking a pair of sunglasses into the shirt pocket and talking over her shoulder to Maxine, who was advising her to take along sandwiches and something to drink. Ralph hardly glanced at Alison, not daring to show his growing feeling of possession.

Lillian and Susie had been out most of the night and were still fast asleep. Ralph could hear Judy's solid footsteps on the floor above, however, and in a moment she came down the steps and into the lobby. He noticed that she seemed to have lost weight and the straight, solid line of her body was beginning to curve in at her waist. He wondered if she had been seeing the woman from the Town Bar.

Alison, feminine despite the severity of her clothing, smiled a casual good morning to Ralph, and Maxine said hello with a friendliness that startled him. He wondered if he had been so wrapped up in his own misery that he had failed to see the new and changed Maxine. He had been watching her, true, but he had been seeking only her bad points, her weaknesses. A twinge of conscience hit him and he felt himself flush with annoyance. He turned and led the way out to the car. They would grab a bite to eat at the airport, he said.

The morning was warm but the airfield proved windy, with dust and sand blowing along the black asphalt. Ralph drove along a dirt road paralleling the runway and turned off beside a red hangar with a big green 3 on its side. An old man stepped around the corner and smiled at them from behind the stem of a corncob pipe.

Ralph and Alison got out, the man took the camera bag, slinging it over his shoulder, and the three of them walked toward the front of the hangar. Coffee and sandwiches made up their breakfast; then Ralph and Alison followed the old man to a black helicopter into which they all climbed. Maxine, who was still sitting in the car, called from the window in the manner of an anxious mother, telling them to be sure to phone the minute they got back. Alison nodded assurance and waved. The blades began spinning and, like a giant grasshopper, the machine leaped into the air and lurched forward.

They traveled low over the rocky terrain and in just a few minutes Ralph saw the giant crab claws of Kinderman hugging the shore. Alison craned to see the water and it was not long before the white foam marking the reef came into view. Ralph glanced at her and saw a smile of pleasure playing at the corners of her mouth. The dark glasses hid her eyes and he had to guess at her mood from the smile, but it left little to his imagination.

He moved closer to take her hand, then thought better of it. The bearded ancient might happen to make a remark to the wrong person.

The helicopter landed on a wide stretch of sand. Ralph climbed out, then held Alison's hand as she jumped to the ground. He took the bag of equipment from the old man's outstretched arm. It was exactly ten-thirty.

"Be back about four," Ralph yelled over the roar of the engine and the old man nodded. They watched the machine rise and head back toward the mainland.

"Well," Ralph said, feeling a little awkward, "this is where we came in."

She laughed, a moment's nostalgia flitting across her face.

"Not quite," she said. "Too many clothes."

He nodded. "And cameras."

Ralph did not quite know how to handle the situation—Alison and he finally alone on the island again. He wished he had thought it through. Nothing for it, he guessed, but to get down to business. He bent over the case and opened the lid. Alison watched him in silence.

"Worst thing in the world to work on the sand," he mumbled for lack of something better to say. "The grains get into the lens rings or scratch the glass. It can get real messy."

"Well, then, let's move up," she said simply.

He paused, caught in the gross inanity of his own conversation. "I guess we ought to," he said and closed the case. They moved up the beach to the ridges of coral. "This is a little better," he said, awkwardly setting down the bag. He knew his comment was unnecessary.

The strong sunshine and the immobility of his subject matter made the shooting a cinch. No need to fuss with shutter and diaphragm openings and light meters. Just lift the Leica, turn slowly on his heel and bang off a series of frames. Then move on to the next spot.

After the tenth set of shots, Alison said simply, "You didn't need me."

For a moment he stood still, the camera held at face level. He looked at her through the view-finder. "Sure I needed you," he said. "Otherwise I'd still be over there in the sand."

She shook her head stubbornly. "You didn't need me," she said again.

He watched her for signs of anger but there were none. Just the simple, straightforward statement, to what purpose he did not know.

"All right," he said. "I wanted you."

"Still?"

"Yes," he challenged. "Still. I'll always want you. You know that. And anyway, it's a pretty lonely island, with nothing but crabs for company."

She took off her glasses and toyed aimlessly with them. Without looking at him, she said, "I don't understand you. You must know what's happening." She hesitated, studying the sand at her feet. "How can it not make any difference to you?"

Ralph closed the case over the camera and fastened the strap before he answered her. "Don't you know that nothing could possibly make any difference in my feelings for you? Nothing."

He did not move to touch her. He wanted her to know that he would wait. He would wait until she needed him as he needed her. She had once. She would again.

He forced himself to fuss with the camera. He had to let her know that she, as a person, was necessary to him, that she was not just a nice piece of flesh brought along to sate his hunger. He wanted her to feel his companionship, his friendship and his love. She had to realize that he was more, for her, than just another man, and certainly more than any woman could ever be.

They climbed along the corals. She put on her glasses again and he turned occasionally to catch the green reflection slanted along her cheekbones. She seemed to know when he needed a special filter or a different lens, for she always had the right one ready in her hand before he turned to ask for it. A large part of the success of the enterprise would depend upon the visual plan he presented to the architect. She must realize this. He was no longer a piece of excess baggage but a key figure in the destiny of Maxine's multi-million-dollar scheme.

He tried to be objective and to think for a moment of what Alison might want for herself if she were beseiged by neither Maxine nor himself. It was peculiar, but he could not envision her being happy in freedom. She seemed to come to life only in response to someone else's desire. And that someone else by all rights was himself.

Although the work was tedious and the climbing slow, Ralph had shot thirty-six frames by three o'clock. They had covered all angles of the island. With everything packed away carefully, they sat down to rest and relax under the shade of a small ledge.

Ralph sat with his equipment beside him, his legs stretched out, wiping the perspiration from his forehead. Alison took out

half a dozen sandwiches and a canteen. Ralph accepted a sand-
wich from her and removed the waxed paper that was wrapped
around it. "In the States," he said casually, "you could have earned
a hundred bucks for your services today." He took a bite, chewing
as he smiled at her with his eyes.

She unscrewed the cap from the canteen and took a long
drink. "You intend to pay me?"

"No joke, Alison. This was a rough bit of work today and I
wish there were some way of thanking you." He crumpled the
waxed paper into a ball and threw it across the sand. Indeed,
he did wish there were something he could give her—but only
something that no one else could give. Somehow he felt awfully
useless. Was he just another man on the fringe of her life, trying
to break into the core?

She noticed the sincerity of his tone and lapsed into a sym-
pathetic silence. He was not at all sure that he liked sympathy
from her. He would have preferred a little temper and noise and
rebellion. Completely forgetting his decision not to touch her, he
leaned forward suddenly and grabbed her shoulders. He heard
the canteen fall as he pulled her to him, her head flung back and
her lips parted. He ran his mouth down her neck, shutting his
eyes and going dizzy with the warm, sweet taste of her skin. He
opened her shirt and slid his hand in to feel her breasts, the soft
flesh of the nipples hardening to his touch. His fingers pulled at
the buckle of her belt.

The faint whirr of a motor came to him from high in the air.
He knew they could not be seen but the sound somehow stripped
him raw. Cursing, he kissed her quickly, furiously, on the mouth
and withdrew his weight from her body.

They watched the helicopter settle onto the sandy beach. He
stood up and held out his hand to her. He noticed that her face
was flushed.

"Take a raincheck?" he asked hopefully.

She picked up the gadget bag and checked the lock. She did not answer but he heard her catch her breath. Then, with two feet of space between them, they made their way across the sand.

Flying back to the mainland, Ralph stared out of the window, making a mental list of all the things he owed her ... in addition to two interrupted lays. First of all, the freedom to make up her own mind. He promised that to himself. When he took her away from Maxine, she must be given enough time to realize herself as an individual. He would hold the other bastards at bay and restrain himself until she was straightened out.

Instead of the whole crew as he had expected, only Basil and the limousine were there to greet them when they landed. He thought that Maxine probably could not stand the smell of sweat. During the ride back to the hotel, he tried in vain to shake off a nasty mood that grew inside of him. He was beginning to feel urgently possessive about Alison and more than a trifle vindictive toward Maxine. He had never regarded the world as a place where you clipped soap coupons in exchange for happiness and long life. Neither had he been used to seeking revenge or doing dirt for the sake of gaining the upper hand. But hatred of Maxine and all that she stood for had been growing in him for a long time. It colored his thoughts and he looked at the world through a haze of male outrage and indignation.

He knew it for what it was but he could do nothing to change what he felt. This hatred was the other side of the coin, directly opposite to his feeling for Alison.

Basil brought the car into the motel's gravel driveway. Almost before the car had stopped, Alison opened the door and jumped out. He was surprised as he watched her run through the entrance into the lobby. She had been sitting beside him so quietly that he had almost forgotten her presence. With a sigh, he opened the door on his side and, lugging the equipment with him, got out. He felt an urgent need to clean the sun and sand from his body. His skin was dry and tight across his face.

As he walked into the lobby, Susie called hello to him and pointed to the ceiling above her with a long forefinger. He nodded. The air-conditioning felt cold inside his head and a small hammer was beginning to pound behind his eyes. He swallowed the dryness in his throat and headed upstairs to the office.

Judy, Lillian and Maxine were waiting for him. It irritated him to see their comfort. He set the bag down on Judy's desk and pulled out the rolls of film, tossing them into Maxine's lap. He saw her hand clutch around one cartridge and then relax.

"I take it this is complete?" she asked, lining the rolls across her fingers.

"That's right," he answered. He went to the bar and poured himself half a glass of brandy. He thought for probably the millionth time that he was drinking too much. With a careless shrug, he drained the glass and put it back on the bar. "If you ladies don't mind," he said on his way to the door, "I'm going to get dressed for the evening." He made a gesture of goodbye and was gone before a comment could be made.

Ralph had some unfinished business to attend to and his mind was occupied with it. Surely Alison would be expecting him. She must realize now that he was no longer an extra in her life. She simply had to come to terms with him—and with herself.

In the privacy of his room, Ralph stripped off his gritty clothes and took a long, cold shower, letting the needle spray pound across his shoulders. He thought about Ali son's leaving the car in such a hurry and wondered where she had gone. She had not gone to Maxine. Apparently she had not wanted to go to Maxine. Perhaps she had wanted to be alone with her thoughts, to compare her feelings for the woman to her feelings for him. He wished he was with her, helping her, letting her know that what she felt for him was right and good.

Briskly he rubbed himself dry and put on a clean white polo shirt and a pair of light blue slacks. Maxine had seen to it that his closet and bureau were filled. There was nothing he lacked in the way of clothing. There was always plenty of food and liquor. Only money was withheld from him. Even cartons of cigarettes were stacked on his dresser so that he would not need small change.

He splashed some after-shave lotion on his skin, brushed back the damp strands of his hair, streaked white by the sun, and set out in search of Alison. Six steps down the hall he saw Judy coming toward him.

"Well, gorgeous, you are the hero of the day," she said. She patted his arm and grinned. "So you are entitled to an extra special dinner all alone with Tarzan." She slapped her chest. "How about it?"

"Sounds great," Ralph said as he linked his arm through hers and they strolled together down the corridor toward the stairs. "Meet you in, say," he glanced at his watch, "an hour and we'll stuff."

"Hour!" Judy exploded. "What do you think I am, a martyr? You look ready and, believe me, I am."

They had already passed Alison's door. Ralph lingered with Judy at the edge of the stairway. "You know how it is," he said. "I got me a mission."

Judy pursed her mouth and shook her head slowly from side to side. "Oh, honey, why don't you give it up? Pick on somebody your own size."

"I know my size when I see it."

She accepted the cigarette he offered her and took out her lighter. "Taking any bets?"

"Nope," he bantered, "I don't like such easy money." He leaned against the bannister, smoking his cigarette, waiting for her to go on her way.

She stood on the top step and looked at him. "Be smart, Ralph, and come have a nice, neutral steak. I know plenty of people in this town. I'll introduce you around. You could get interested somewhere on more favorable territory, if that's what you need. Where the battleground isn't, shall we say, so limited."

Ralph flicked an ash over his shoulder and down the stairwell. "You don't know everything I know," he said easily. How could she possibly know that Alison had responded to him with a passion that matched his own? Judy probably thought the girl had turned away from him in disgust.

"Ralph, you're much too smart to be this confident," Judy insisted, her tone suddenly serious. "Maybe you're making things up without realizing it?"

"So now I'm nuts?"

"No," she said, "just mixed up."

Two tall men with blonde pompadours came up the stairs together, chuckling, blue turkish towels hanging from their sunburned shoulders. They brushed past Ralph, nodded a greeting to Judy.

Ralph waited until they had entered a room and closed the door behind them. "If you'll pardon me," he said, "this isn't exactly what you'd call a fair conversation. Could be that I have private info."

He was unprepared for Judy's laugh. It flatly accused him of childishness or stupidity or both.

"Laugh away, old girl," he said, annoyed.

"Oh, heck," Judy said impatiently. "Can't you see that I'm just trying to keep this one big, happy family? And here you are doing somersaults because ... well ... I suppose because she kissed you or something."

"Or something."

"I don't know what it is with you," she said. She rubbed her neck and turned to lean on the other elbow. "How come a smart guy like you can't figure out where sex belongs in the scheme of things? Since when can you lead a girl around by her orgasms?"

It was Ralph's turn to laugh. His composure returned and he began to feel secure again. "And you're a doctor?" he kidded.

"Was," Judy corrected.

"So be it," he shrugged. "But please don't try selling me fairy tales." He looked at his watch and began edging into the hall toward Alison's room.

"Well, will you listen a minute?" she asked. She put a hand on his arm to detain him.

"Okay, but keep it simple." He was looking around for a place to put the cigarette butt.

"Just drop it." She put the sole of her shoe on the butt and rubbed it out. "Now that I've got the podium, I don't quite know how to say it."

"Just spit."

"Well, what I mean is," she said slowly, "I suppose, that you just quit fooling yourself. That's all. It's pretty obvious, isn't it, that Alison has made up her mind to stay with Max? I don't know if it's love or not, but she believes that Max needs her and that settles it as far as Alison is concerned." She sighed. "What's the use? If I have to spell it out for you, it's no good." She started down the stairs. "But just the same," she said over her shoulder, "you'll be missing a darned good steak."

Ralph watched her slowly descend the stairs. Then he wondered why she had bothered to try to deter him. She must have known that his interest in Alison was not something that he could lightly brush away. Or maybe she was just worried about Maxine's status? Of course. That must be it. And that was just fine. He had been right. Alison was having doubts that nobody wanted to admit.

From the head of the stairs, Ralph looked down the long corridor with its full length windows at both ends. A cough sounded in one of the rooms, breaking the stillness for a moment, then all was quiet again. Judy had herself a sweet proposition here, he thought. She made more money than she would have ever made as a doctor. Yet he often sensed in her the restlessness of her frustrated ideals. She easily could have bought her license back and set up a practice right here in town, but that kind of a compromise was not for her. Why the hell couldn't she allow him as much integrity?

Yet he could not put her admonition out of his mind. Despite her own leanings, Judy, as a doctor, should have been the first to encourage Alison to seek satisfaction in a normal love relationship. The girl's response to his love-making had been strong and sincere. She had reacted with a fervor and passion that made his blood race every time he thought about it.

He hesitated before Alison's door, remembering Judy's words. Then, with sudden decision, he knocked determinedly. The hollow sound echoed inside. He waited, then he knocked again, but he knew in his heart that the room was empty. He felt the vacuum in it. So this was going to be the grand chase tonight, was it? He wondered if Judy had known that Alison was not in her room. Had Maxine outsmarted him again? It was just possible that she had, the bitch. With her around, almost anything was possible.

There was nothing else for him to do but to search for Judy in hopes of resuming their casual banter. He sauntered down the stairs and around the lobby, hoping to find her in conversation with some of the guests. Outside, in the parking lot in front of the hotel, he spotted her leaning against the side of a red Jowett and speaking to Maxine with wild gestures of her hands. Just how obvious can you get? he wondered.

It was Maxine who saw him and motioned to him eagerly with a gloved hand. To his surprise, her face was relaxed and she appeared genuinely glad to see him. He waited for her to speak first.

"I had a glance at the negatives in the darkroom while they were still wet," she explained pleasantly. "Apparently you were quite thorough. We'll have the enlargements tomorrow and you can get down to business with the architects. Thank you." Her gratitude was sincere.

Judy idly swung the car door back and forth against her hip and listened. She looked from Maxine's face to Ralph's and back again with what was supposed to represent an impersonal interest.

Ralph pulled the door from her hand and swung himself into the seat next to Maxine. "If you really want to thank me," he said, "drive me around in this nice evening breeze." He slammed the door shut.

Caught off guard, Maxine laughed. "Sure, if you'd like." She looked at Judy. "Join us?"

"No, thanks. I'm still on my way to dinner. Been trying to get there for over an hour now." She smiled a little uneasily. "But try to get along without me." She waved and stepped away from the car as Maxine turned the key and started the motor.

Ralph laughed to himself at the obvious concern on Judy's face. Poor thing, she would never make a good actress—she was too simple and honest by nature. And she would probably choke on her steak, wondering what the devil he was up to.

Maxine swerved the car around and drove away from the sun. She handled the speedster with ease, her left elbow resting lightly on the rolled-down window.

"If I could only pay all my debts so simply." She smiled at him. Ralph felt strangely at ease with her now. He sat back and studied her without emotion, trying to fathom her weaknesses. He noticed that the reddish brown arms were sleek with muscle.

She obviously felt like talking and he let her. She kept her eyes on the road, glancing occasionally in the rearview mirror.

"You know," she said impulsively, "this little plan is going so well, I can hardly believe that it's mine."

Indeed, he thought. She had never struck him as the kind of person who got things easily. She was a fighter and she must have been so all her life. He realized that her new informality, the ready smile, the friendly confidences, were only surface traits, and he knew better than to let down his guard.

"If it continues this way, we should be in the moneymaking business by next February." She spoke more to herself than to him.

"I don't see why not," he said. "Everyone seems to be pitching in for the common good." He did not want to disturb the trend of her thoughts by disagreeing with her in any way, nor did he want her to become aware of him by his silence. Best, he thought, to echo gently with little comment.

She wiped a speck from the windshield. "Yes, isn't it marvelous luck? I had expected to run into all sorts of complications. Instead, everything seems to be falling into place almost by itself."

"I can hardly imagine what kind of complications there could be," he said. "You people have access to plenty of money and certainly to the best contacts. How could it be anything but successful?"

She smiled. "My boy," she said, "there are always complications." Her tone was low and full of the memories of uglier days. Suddenly he wondered where Alison was.

"Oh, well," he said casually. He was looking away from her, watching the early moon nestle between two twilight clouds. "You don't expect the good things of life to be handed over on a silver platter. Even your … er … your niece enjoys a good hassle now and then."

He had expected Maxine to stiffen and become defensive but she laughed with warmth and, glancing quickly at her face, he knew she meant to be friendly.

"She's plenty stubborn, all right," she said. The affection she had for the girl was obvious in her tone and in the soft lines around her eyes. "If we could build the resort on her temperament, it would last longer than the island. Just try to argue with her some time. She's got a special technique that I guarantee you is invincible. Kind of a passive resistance. Quiet, acquiescent on the surface. It's a real experience, trying to get her to change her mind."

Ralph listened to her as she spoke at length about Alison. She spoke with such evident relish and openness that one might have thought they were mother and daughter. It made Ralph distinctly uncomfortable. He felt like a Peeping Tom treated to a keyhole view. He wanted to shut Maxine up, to shout her down with the side of Alison he knew, that he alone knew. Miserably he realized that Maxine would not talk so freely if she considered him any kind of a threat.

Then he remembered suddenly what Judy had said. Apparently Alison had pledged her allegiance to Maxine so fervently that the woman felt no reason to be insecure.

Just as he thought he could not bear another minute of listening to her, Maxine lapsed into silence. He yearned to put in a dig, a tiny needle, to burst the balloon of her joy.

"And where's the protégé tonight?" He studied the sea as it blended with the darkening sky.

"There's an old Garbo picture playing in town that Lillian insisted upon seeing. Alison and Susie tagged along to make it a threesome." Maxine glanced over her shoulder, then made a sharp U-turn. "We've been loafing along like this so we can pick them up in an hour." She tilted the sunshade to cut off the last rays of the setting sun. "I thought you knew."

"Oh, that's right," he lied. "I forgot."

His heart sank. How could she? How could she have rushed off to a silly, inconsequential movie when she had every reason to suppose that he would be looking for her? The thoughtlessness of it stabbed at him relentlessly—and then he suddenly realized that Maxine had been waiting for her at the same time. That was it! Alison had felt trapped and her only way out had been to accompany Lillian to the movies. He could scarcely keep from laughing out loud. The poor kid. He hoped she had at least enjoyed the film.

CHAPTER TEN

DURING THE hour that they dawdled along the highway, Ralph found many more reasons, and all of them flattering to himself, as to why Alison preferred going to a movie to seeing him. He favored the idea that she had escaped into safe territory because she was afraid to trust herself alone with him, especially since the afternoon's unfinished episode.

It comforted him a little to saturate his mind with this image of her as the weak, feminine woman. She would run blindly from the reality of her growing desires until they became too strong for her to resist, and once she had made the choice for herself, she would, he hoped, belong completely to him.

He caught only bits and snatches of Maxine's chatter. It was no longer necessary for him to know her views of Alison. Only one thing was of any concern to him. He must have Alison all to himself—and very soon. Then they could leave the hideous resort. It was absolutely essential, however, that Maxine's enterprise be successful since Alison's pity for the woman's predicament was a much stronger link in her attachment than she herself realized.

The hour finally passed and Maxine parked in front of the movie house. Ralph was beginning to feel a little self-conscious and just the least bit apprehensive. He lit another cigarette, hiding behind the screen of smoke and trying to put a brake on his mounting tension. Probably Alison would be nonchalant and he must be too. He managed to be turned to Maxine, making small talk, when the door was opened behind him.

"Superb!" Lillian breathed, her eyes closed for the full length of the word. "Just superb! There can never be another like her."

Ralph said, "Hi," to all three, giving no more heed to Alison than to any of the others. He got out and pushed the back of the seat forward so they could climb into the rear of the car.

"She makes me so sad," said Susie, flufling her skirt into the proper ruffles. "I couldn't stand to be so all alone with myself and depressed like that. You would think she'd live and dance a little in just one of her pictures, but she never does."

Maxine laughed and waited until Ralph got in and closed the door. "Would you gals like something liquid to wash away all this soulfulness?"

Susie said, "I could just go for an ice cream soda."

"For heaven's sake, girl, have you nothing sensitive in your soul?" Lillian exclaimed.

"I was plenty sensitive when it came to helping you get your divorce."

Ralph turned in his seat. "Come, come, children," he said. "No quarreling." He took advantage of the moment to look deliberately at Alison. She was listening with amusement to the bickering, her eyes moving from Susie's face to Lillian's as they spoke. Ralph's glance did not catch her attention and she seemed no more aware of his presence than did the others.

He had not expected semaphore signals but at least she could have given him some sign of recognition, a gesture or a smile meant for him alone. She merely seconded the motion for ice cream sodas. He had the feeling that she was deliberately ignoring him.

Ralph spent the rest of the evening in hurt resentment, forcing a show of good nature that he was far from feeling. He did not sleep until the dawn was streaking the sky. He glared bleakly into the darkness of his room, more determined than ever to smash the bonds that kept his Alison captive.

He slept until after ten and awoke feeling stiff and disagreeable. Breakfast tasted lousy, the first cigarettes were lousy, the whole damned world was lousy. He had the feeling that it just wasn't going to be his day.

Maxine entered the kitchen as he was helping himself to a second cup of strong, black coffee. She seemed very chipper. "Whenever you're ready," she said, "we'll be off to the architects."

He swirled the hot liquid around in his mouth and swallowed it. Let her wait, dammit. He wasn't ready yet. In fact, he might not be ready for a couple of hours. What the devil was she so happy about these days, anyway? He had liked it better when the cannon had been firing. At least a guy knew where he stood that way.

He dawdled with the coffee and lit a cigarette that he did not want. It tasted like burned rope. He slumped back against the chair and spewed smoke into the air, but she remained unruffled. He could not irritate her.

The coffee, the lousy coffee, settled his disposition somewhat and he realized that it was not to his advantage to try to delay her. These things had to be done sooner or later, and the sooner the ball was rolling, the sooner Alison would be his.

He was wearing cream-colored slacks and a dark blue shirt unbuttoned at the neck. In a little while he would be escorted across a plush office by gentlemen in suits and ties. But Maxine, if she noticed at all, mentioned nothing about his appearance as she walked beside him to the lobby.

Both Judy and Alison were waiting for them. And both said good morning to him as pleasantly and as impersonally as if he were just another guest at the motel. He nodded curtly in reply. What irked Ralph was not so much the coldness of the greeting but his complete inability to catch any undercurrents.

Ralph turned off the highway into town and drove along a wide boulevard where young palm trees lined the sidewalks.

"Who has the pictures?" Judy asked.

"They were sent down to the office early this morning. I checked by phone." Maxine patted a whisp of hair into place.

When they arrived, Ralph held open the paneled door labeled WHITNEY BROS., ARCHITECTS and the women filed in. He let it close against his shoulders and found himself in a large combination work-and-reception room decorated in teak and stainless steel. Spread out on a wide table top were the enlargements of Ralph's photographs. A red-haired man looked up as they entered and came quickly from behind the desk.

"I'm so glad you could arrange to come down so early," he said. His voice had an excited, almost breathless, quality that grated on Ralph's nerves. "This project is most fascinating. I am anxious to discuss it with you." He seemed to know all three of the women and he led them forward to teakwood chairs arranged around the desk. Then he caught sight of Ralph and paused. "I'm sorry," his voice took on a polite edge of reserve, "but I don't believe we've met."

Maxine said quickly, "This is Ralph Thayer, our general manager. He took the pictures. Mr. Thayer, I'd like you to meet Alexis Whitney, who can build anything anywhere, with dispatch and efficiency."

"I am pleased to meet you, Mr. Thayer," Whitney said, stepping forward and taking Ralph's hand in a firm grip. He inclined his head slightly and studied Ralph's face with unabashed openness as though he were used to doing exactly as he pleased. Quickly he found another chair for Ralph. Then he scooped up the pictures and began to put them in order. "Now, if I am not mistaken," he said, turning his glance again to Maxine, "if I am not mistaken, you want a large house and as many bungalow-type dwellings as it is possible to erect on this ground space."

"Yes," Maxine said.

"Well, then, first, let us go over these pictures together and make sure that I have the layout of the island correct in my mind."

"Mr. Thayer and myself are the only ones who can help you with that," Alison volunteered.

"Well, if you please." Whitney had moved around his desk and was covering the glass top with rows of pictures.

Ralph picked up a ballpoint pen, put the pictures in proper order and numbered them. With himself on one side of the man and Alison on the other, he took particular delight in the fact that Maxine and Judy were, for a change, left out. He felt once more as though he were sharing something intensely personal with Alison.

Whitney, engrossed in the project, was busy with another pen and a large sheet of paper as he outlined levels and asked for ground measurements. Ralph had to remind him at one point that he was a photographer and not an engineer. The man nodded and apologized, then proceeded to ask questions that were even more technical.

Ralph made a point of consulting Alison about certain things he pretended had slipped his mind. He wanted to highlight clearly the exclusiveness of their experience together. He asked her to describe in minute detail many secluded spots, indicating to the others that he and Alison had spent much time alone there. He noticed that she was slightly flushed and that when she looked at him, her eyes were tender.

Whitney listened attentively, now and then tapping his lower lip with the small finger of his left hand, squinting his eyes every so often as though to bring into focus the image coming to life in his brain. Abruptly he pulled a sheaf of drawing paper from the top drawer of the desk. He sketched swiftly and surely, the pencil moving cleanly across the page.

"Something along this line, perhaps?"

Maxine stepped forward and looked down at the sketch as though it were a sacred scripture. The others gathered around to peer over her shoulder.

"You see," Whitney explained, indicating penciled lines with the tip of his finger, "there are very few extended flat levels. The bungalows will have to be molded to fit into the rocks, so to speak. We won't be able to do much leveling but we can be pretty safe in assuming a fair number of split-level dwellings."

Judy nodded. "I guess it will be whatever you say, Alex."

Whitney pushed a button and the lights over the wide desk dimmed. "Well, fine. I think it's going to be a very beautiful and unusual bit of work." He smiled. "And, since you have assured me that a boat large enough to carry materials and equipment can get in, in addition to the fact that we will have a helicopter at our service constantly, I think we will eventually give you exactly what you want."

The three women thanked him for his enthusiasm and assured him of their confidence. Ralph waited impatiently while they took a lengthy and wordy leave, with Whitney promising to phone them just as soon as he had prepared a preliminary draft.

CHAPTER ELEVEN

THERE WAS no conversation among them on the way back to the hotel or, for that matter, during the rest of the afternoon. Maxine seemed completely withdrawn, radiating an aura of deep thoughtfulness. Judy and Alison looked at her, then at each other, and decided to leave her in peace. Later in the afternoon, Alison went out to the terrace and found Maxine sitting on a beach chair, staring out at the ocean and unaware of the smile on her lips. Alison fetched one of Judy's peaked fishing caps and pulled it down over the silvered head. Maxine did not even look up.

"She's gone daft," Alison remarked. "Her face will burn to a crisp and that'll be the end of Whitney's assignment."

Ralph sat near Maxine, smoking cigarette after cigarette, and creating a few private dreams of his own. If Maxine would remain in her state of euphoria, he knew his own plans could be carried off without a hitch. And if Alison had not been able to penetrate Maxine's preoccupation, there was little chance that Maxine would even know he was alive.

The plan of action he had mapped out for himself was fairly simple. First he would suggest to Maxine that, as a safety measure before blasting the channel, they should make a movie of the underwater approach to the island. Alison, who was a fine underwater swimmer and already knew the way, would of course go with him. He knew that Maxine would not object to anything that might insure the success of her venture. Nor, in her present state of mind, would she think twice about his real motives. And, from previous experience, he figured that Alison would be glad to go along if only for the promise of adventure.

He would have to go to Kinderman and arrange with Clara to have a motorboat ready near the island. He and Alison could be taken out to the reef by Noah and they would send him away with instructions to return in four hours. Once Noah was gone, Ralph would somehow manage to get Alison into the smaller boat with him and head back to Kinderman. One way or the other, he had to go to Kinderman to pick up the thousand dollars from Ed and he had to do it at the last minute so that Montrose would not have a chance to talk.

And if they could manage to reach the mainland without any trouble, they could hire a car to take them to the airport. In a matter of hours they could be on a plane—any plane going anywhere. It didn't matter where.

The long afternoon wore on, Maxine and Ralph each involved in his own dreams. Alison, who soon became bored with both of them, ran carelessly at the edge of the foam, soaking her leather sandals and the salmon-colored shorts that clung to her thighs. When she was bored with that too, she ran back to the terrace and settled herself in the shade of a tree.

Ralph wanted desperately to join her but he did not dare take any chances with Maxine now. There was too much at stake. The woman might at any moment awaken from her reverie and thrust herself between them. Even at the risk of Alison's misunderstanding his behavior, he must not aggravate Maxine. Yet, if she truly loved Alison, why couldn't she realize that the girl would be better off away from this life, from the shadowy fringes of society? Maybe when she really became involved in the building of the resort, she would lose interest in the girl. For her own good, Ralph hoped that Maxine would be able in time to forget Alison.

When the sun began to disappear behind the palm trees, Maxine bestirred herself and stood up. She pulled off the silly cap and dropped it with a smile on the chair. Alison had gone indoors for a jacket. Judy had long ago gone off for a sail with Lillian and Susie.

For a while Maxine looked across the beach, watching the sand form into slanting hills in response to the fingers of the wind. "We should have invited Whitney out here tonight," she said with sudden annoyance. "I can't imagine why it didn't occur to me earlier."

Ralph laughed to himself. Lots of things haven't occurred to you, Max.

"I'm going to do that right now," she said with sudden decision. "Why don't you come in with me, Ralph? We'll have something to drink. And maybe you'll come up with some ideas that will be useful." She ran her fingers through her hair and waited for his answer.

"That'll be fine," he said. He got up from the boulder he had been sitting on and followed her indoors. So damned soon, and I didn't even have to do the asking. Is this luck or is this luck! But he managed to keep a calm and impersonal expression on his face.

Upstairs in Judy's den, Ralph lingered over the preparation of the drinks while Maxine went to the phone. She held the receiver to her ear for at least twenty rings, Ralph calculated, before she lowered it back into its cradle.

"God punished me," she said wryly, taking the glass Ralph had prepared for her. She sat in the swivel chair, kicked off her shoes and crossed her feet on the edge of the desk. "That man's a genius. I'd feel brazen as hell if I tried to suggest anything to him."

"Yeah, I know what you mean," Ralph said. "He gives you that feeling." He tossed his pack of cigarettes across the desk to her. "Once he gets on that island, he'll take over like the Marines."

She nodded. "Exactly. I've been sitting out there all day, mulling and thinking and imagining, and I'll be damned if I could come up with anything better than the idea he threw at us in two minutes." A breeze from the open window stirred some papers and she put her foot on top of them. "It's amazing," she said, "but suddenly I have nothing, absolutely nothing, to worry about."

"Except maybe teaching me how to set charges to blast a path through the coral," he said casually. He looked carefully into his glass, then went across the room to refill it.

"I don't understand."

"Well, you said we have to get a boat out to the island. I'm a photographer. I don't know anything about demolition work. How are we going to handle the job?"

She turned her dark eyes to him in honest perplexity. "You know, I honestly hadn't thought about that."

"Okay. So we can start thinking about it now."

She considered for a moment, then gestured helplessly. "Blank," she said. She handed him her glass and motioned for him to pour.

He refilled it and waited for her to drink before continuing. He balanced his own glass on the arm of the chair, using it as a point of focus. She had half finished her drink before he ventured further.

"The only thing that occurs to me as being at all practical," he said, "is to call in a demolition team to do the actual blasting. In the meantime, I can prepare a little so-called visual education for them."

"How do you mean?"

"Well, I went out and took a lot of pictures so Whitney could get the lay of the land," he said. He glanced at her casually, looking for a response. "It seems to me that those pictures were pretty valuable to him."

"True."

"Without the snaps, he couldn't have begun to know what kind of building the place would take."

"Yes," she nodded.

"Well, is there any reason we can't proceed the same way with cutting the channel? I can take a small movie camera with me and photograph the actual path into the lagoon that the boat will eventually take. The film would then be reeled off a few times for whoever's doing the job and he'd be almost as familiar with the set-up as I am."

She sat for a moment in silence, tasting the alcohol and watching the flutter of the papers beneath her heel. "You know," she said, "that sounds pretty good. Yes, that's very good."

"It'll just take a few hours," he went on. "Nothing can go wrong. Alison will swim with me and carry some extra lighting. The whole thing will be a cinch and we'll have it done in no time." He snapped his fingers and forced a smile. How little she realized the truth.

"You know, I think I'll be sorry to see you go. Back to the States, I mean." She drained the contents of the glass and swung around to face the window.

His stomach plunged. "Back to the States?"

"Sure," she said, her back still to him. "How can I keep you here forever? You have a fiancée waiting for you. You have a life of your own. Just stay until the job is running smoothly and then you can pack off for home."

His eyes narrowed and he was glad she was not facing him. So that was her game, was it? She had decided to get rid of him, had she? Decided he was too dangerous to have around after all? Well, he'd be leaving, all right. And wouldn't she be surprised to discover that Alison had gone with him?

"It's just as well," he said. "Peggy's probably getting pretty impatient."

She swung around to face him and set the glass down on the desk with a clink. "Enough said. Why don't you go write and tell her to be watching the airports?"

His wariness started to abate somewhat and he began to feel calm again. He would stick with the original plan, of course, but he really did owe Peggy a letter of explanation and this was probably as good a time as any to write it. "You're right," he said. He stood up and edged toward the door. "I will drop her a line."

He went downstairs and took paper and an envelope from one of the small writing desks in the lobby. Then he went up to his room and tried to think of what he could say that would hurt her the least. He started the letter six times before he found the words that best satisfied him.

Dear Peggy,

What I have to say will not come as a surprise to you for it has been in the wind for many years. Still, it has not been easy to find just the right words. Probably you could find them more easily, for your grievances against me must be many. Anyway, what I have to say will probably come as a relief to you. ...

He read through the letter several times and he felt a greater warmth and tenderness toward her than he had in years. He hoped that she would eventually find someone who could be for her all that he had failed to be. And yet, he thought as he sealed the envelope, what a relief it was to be free.

He sauntered casually into the office where Maxine was hunched over the desk, engrossed in columns of figures on a large white sheet of paper. Ralph waved the envelope at her.

"Done," he said. "Now, just for the record, I'm going to drive into town and drop it off at the post office."

Maxine looked up, her eyes strangely clear. Apparently the alcohol had taken no effect. She nodded absently, then returned to the column of figures. He closed the door quietly behind him, a secret smile flitting across his face.

He found the little black Austin without trouble, climbed in behind the wheel and headed toward town. He would not be able to do more than fifty in the little car, he knew, but there was really no need to hurry. He had everything so well under control that nothing could possibly go wrong. The post office was on the way to the ocean road. He stopped long enough to shove the letter through a slot, then turned west along the water. He figured he could easily make it to Kinderman in an hour.

Whisps of fog drifted in through the window and brushed his face with dampness. The paved road soon gave way to the rutted wagon path they had traveled with Montrose. He could barely see where he was going. He knew he had reached the town when he heard the slap of water against the pier. He wiped the windshield with his sleeve, squinting up the hill in the direction of the hotel. No one saw him. Good. He did not want to be recognized.

Ralph parked the Austin and went into one of the bars along the waterfront. He peered at the faces of the natives hunched along the bar. He was looking for one in particular—a man with a guitar to whom he had once given a bottle in a moment of drunken generosity.

The man was seated alone at a table near the back, rolling a cigarette. Ralph slid into the seat next to him and touched his sleeve. The whisky-bleared eyes looked at him coldly for a minute, then they narrowed in recognition. The man nodded. Ralph leaned toward him confidentially, put his arm around his shoulders and beckoned him closer with a crooked finger.

Deliberately he spoke with a drunken lisp. The fellow cocked his head and listened intently. "You know Clara?" Ralph asked.

"Clara?" the man repeated. His eyes brightened. He nodded his head in affirmation.

"Where does she live?"

The face crumpled up with an understanding smile. The man nodded happily. He took Ralph's arm and they got up from the table. He pulled Ralph outside and pointed up the hill. Ralph looked at him questioningly and, without hesitation, the native led him up the stony path until they were opposite a hovel almost hidden behind a small clump of bushes.

"Thanks." Ralph turned his pockets inside out.

The man understood and smiled again, putting his hands up in protest. Hurriedly he backed away down the hill into the mist.

Ralph turned to examine Clara's house. Through a small rectangle cut high in the side, he saw the flickering of an orange flame playing against the inside wall. He did not know how many there were in Clara's family or, indeed, if he would even find her there.

He picked his way across twisted roots and stones to the warped wooden door. Clara herself answered his knock. She was barefoot and wore a skirt of brightly printed cloth. She looked at him for a long minute before she recognized him, then her huge lips parted in a wide smile. "Mother Earth protects her own," she said.

He smiled back at her. "Can I come in, Clara? I want to talk to you."

She held the door open for him and he entered.

Three young children sat on the mat-covered floor, their eyes blinking sleepily, their faces turned to the warmth of the fireplace. A single table and two chairs furnished the room. He sat down on one of the chairs and waited for her to join him.

"I am alone here with *los niños*," she said. "You can speak free. My husband is out yet, cleanin' and fixin' fish."

He might just as well come straight out with it, he decided, and let her take it from there. "Clara, I want you to do me some favors." He leaned forward on his elbows and looked into her eyes. "If you will help me, I can get away to my own country. If you don't, I will have to stay here. A prisoner."

Clara drew her eyebrows together, making deep furrows across her forehead. "What you mean, prisoner?" she said suspiciously. "You're not a boss man?"

He knew that to be too detailed would only cause confusion and so he kept to the bare essentials. "I'm no boss man without money," he said. "Montrose has my money. I want you to help me get it back from him."

She put a hand under her blouse and scratched her shoulder. "The dog."

Ralph smiled. "Will you help me?" he urged.

"*Siempre*. What you want me to do?"

He outlined all that had to be done—arranging for the motorboat, clothing, getting the money from Montrose. She listened, blinking her dark eyes from time to time to show him that she understood. Ralph spoke simply and went over the plan again and again to make certain that she grasped it. He was not sure of the time at which he would need the boat nor even of the day. She would have to have the boat ready and waiting for him every day until he could get to it with the girl. When he got his money, he would repay Clara generously for her expenses and her services.

He left, feeling satisfied that she would do her part. She was glad to help him, remembering the years of generous tips he had given her, and she had no qualms whatsoever about doing Montrose dirt.

Driving back was a slow process. The fog was rolling in from the ocean in thick clouds, dense and smothering. He crawled along the road, the window open beside him, his head poked outside to catch the first sound of an approaching vehicle. It was after midnight when he pulled up under the neon lights of The Sportsman.

He relaxed for a moment against the leather seat, then took a quick glance into the rear-view mirror for telltale signs of road dirt. He wiped his face and neck on a handkerchief. He felt grimy all over.

He went upstairs to his room without seeing any of the women. He splashed cold water over his face, arms and hands, combed his hair and put on a fresh shirt. He took a final look at himself in the dresser mirror. There were gray lines in his face, puffy skin under his eyes. God, would he need a rest when this was all over.

Alison was coming up the stairs as he left his room and he met her in the hall. She wore a gray-flannel skirt and a powder-blue sweater and she looked disarmingly innocent and far younger than her nineteen years.

The old aching at the sight of her trembled inside of him and he averted his eyes so that his emotion would not be visible. He struggled for a casual greeting.

"We're going swimming tomorrow," he said. "Movie stuff this time. Hope you'll like it."

She stopped and leaned back against the wall, her hands crossed behind her back. "I heard something to that effect," she said casually. "Didn't know it was tomorrow."

For a minute he did not answer, but searched her face, trying to determine her mood. "Well," he said, "I can't see any reason for putting it off. The sooner, the better, don't you think?"

She met his gaze steadily and held it. There was no expression on her face that he could fathom, but her eyes and her manner were as calm as they had been when he first met her.

He could not restrain himself. All the weeks of waiting, of wanting her, condensed into an immediate burning need for her. He touched his fingertips to her chin and tilted her lips to meet his own. She did not pull away, nor did she cling to him. She simply stood there and let him kiss her.

Disappointed, he stopped and pulled away. "That was unwise of me," he said curtly, "and I'm sorry."

She turned to go on down the hall toward her room. "None of us is unwise," she said. "We just experiment."

He walked beside her down the hall to her room. Neither of them said a word. She stopped in the doorway and turned toward him with her arm stretched across the frame.

He looked down at her and thought how very tired she looked. Why try to force anything now? She was not in the mood.

"Good night," he said abruptly. "Sleep well."

CHAPTER TWELVE

RALPH was awake and dressed before seven, too excited to waste time on sleep. It would be another two hours before the stores opened. He hoped that Maxine would be up early and ready to go with him to get the supplies needed for the trip.

He recognized a touch of irony in the situation, knowing that Maxine herself was making possible the abduction of Alison. This he savored. Maybe some day he would get over the bitterness he felt toward Maxine, might even be able honestly to pity her a bit. But today there was no trace of compassion in him.

At seven-thirty he sauntered out of his room and down the stairs. The lobby was deserted and depressing. He could not stay there alone. He went into the kitchen, deciding that he would wait there for Maxine. He made coffee in an old-fashioned tin pot, carried the pot and a cup to a table and sat down to sip restlessly.

At a little after eight the rest of the troupe joined him. He listened to the chit-chat and tried not to appear anxious. He hoped that Maxine or Alison would say something about the plans for the day. He would be glad for a cue to start things moving. But it was not until after a full breakfast was eaten and they were smoking the morning's first round of cigarettes that Maxine mentioned the expedition. She addressed herself to Judy, who listened thoughtfully. From behind his own cigarette, Ralph watched the round face, but it revealed nothing of the suspicion he had expected to find there.

When Maxine stopped talking in order to light a second cigarette, Ralph said as casually as he could, "I suppose today is as good as any. We really ought to get this thing done as soon as possible so that Whitney won't be delayed."

"How do you mean?" As she spoke, Judy looked directly into his eyes with her frank, open stare. He wondered if she were baiting him.

"You people probably don't realize this," he said, shifting to address the whole group so that he would not have to fence with Judy, "and there's no reason why you should, but it takes a long time to process movie film. Since Whitney is such a fast worker, we'll have to go some to keep ahead of him. He'll be wanting to get out to the island soon, I should think. Of course," he shrugged his shoulders, "if you have a reason to wait, that's up to you."

He was hoping that Alison would support him, but she was apparently absorbed in blowing smoke rings.

"I think you're right," Maxine said decisively. A knowing smile formed around her lips and Ralph realized suddenly that she thought he was in a hurry because of the letter he had written to Peggy. He grinned back at her.

The small exchange of good will had not relaxed Judy, but she said, "Okay. Might as well be today, boy."

Ralph squashed his cigarette into an ash tray. "Well, in that case," he said briskly, "I'd better see about the equipment. We'll need some new diving gear, among other things." He stood up. "Anybody coming with me?"

Maxine and Alison both nodded and followed him to the parking lot. The morning's jaunt was strictly routine. Ralph had a free hand with respect to money, so things went rapidly. It was not quite noon when he stowed the gear and supplies in the trunk of the Austin and the three of them headed back to the motel.

A hot sun had evaporated the night's fog and all of the women decided to go along on the *Jim Boy* for the ride. They made a picnic of it, carrying with them baskets of lunch and bottles of wine in vacuum coolers. Ralph was momentarily annoyed, but he saw no way for them to interfere with his plans and he pretended to be glad to have them along.

Noah nosed the boat away from the pier and out toward the open sea. The water was busy, crowded with craft of all types, ranging from rafts to steam yachts.

Noah made a wide circle away from shore and moved out at a rapid pace that pleased Ralph. He wished he could turn and watch Alison. She sat behind him with her head tilted back, her face into the sun, talking easily with Maxine. The girl did not appear to suspect that within a few hours she would be gone, lost forever to Maxine.

The breeze was brisk, and Ralph's spirits were high. He stood beside Noah, his face to the wind. He remained in his private dream-world until the plop of the anchor broke across his thoughts and only then did he realize that they had reached the edge of the reef.

He turned and went to Alison, who was waiting in a black bikini. He buckled her into an oxygen tank and tested the valves. Standing there in the fins and close-fitting mask, she seemed more delicate, more fragile, than ever before.

It was not until he was shrugging his shoulders into the straps of his own air tanks that he noticed Maxine. She had just stepped out of the cabin, dressed in a tight black suit that emphasized the youthfulness of her body and, like himself and Alison, she was equipped for diving. He felt the muscles of his jaw tense as he watched her approach the rail.

"Let's go," Alison said from behind him.

He turned and looked past her to Judy. She met his look levelly and he saw in her eyes a flicker of defiance. He moved across the deck and stood beside Maxine.

"I hope you don't mind," she said. "I've been dying for a chance to do this. I've never been on the island, you know, and I thought—"

"It's a dangerous swim," he interrupted.

Maxine smiled. "Mr. Thayer," she said calmly, "I dare say you were still in swaddling clothes when I was learning to swim. Alison is a pupil of mine. She does rather well, don't you think?"

He knew that objection would be futile. The woman was determined to go. It was almost as though she had read his mind and knew the details of his plan. Yet he could not determine whether this crimp in his scheme were deliberate on her part or simply a hideous coincidence.

He still had one chance. If Alison would go with him willingly, they could easily lose Maxine among the twisting, narrow crevices in the reef and reach the hidden motorboat before Maxine could work her way back to the open sea. Yes—if Alison would go with him. And willingly.

He shrugged. "Suit yourself."

Noah lowered them over the side into the water. Ralph felt the ocean close over his head and the heavy equipment become suddenly weightless. He motioned to Alison to swim ahead of him and she started the descent, back arched, flippers moving with a steady beat. Maxine followed close behind, moving easily through the water. Ralph clutched the camera and waited to reach the first rows of coral before starting the film.

There was unusual activity among the creatures of the coral reef. Shrimp scurried along rock ledges. Crabs waddled on the bottom in great number. Fish of every variety were scuttling everywhere. It looked as though the reef population had been evicted from its homes and was wandering aimlessly about.

Ralph simply took it for granted that the storm of the day before had stirred up all the activity. He did not stop to really think about it. Concerned only with carrying out his plans, he tried to calculate how long it would take the *Jim Boy* to get safely out of sight on its way back to shore.

Alison had turned on the light and he watched the two figures swimming in front of him. They resembled weird, unearthly, shimmering creatures, moving like stalking predators through the murky water. Ralph smiled to himself. He knew he had not really needed the light, and he felt rather sorry for the poor, frightened fish.

But an undersea world larger than any he had ever seen before was visible to him. He realized that the camera in his hands was recording thousands of dollars worth of material. If he had the film processed himself once they got back to the States he would have not only an excellent documentary film but plenty of stills for articles. There would be more than enough material to fill Ed's assignment and still bring in a sizeable bit of cash from other sources.

Despite himself, he forgot about filming the path through the coral reef, forgot about his other plans, and eagerly turned his view-finder on the sea creatures darting around him. He glanced ahead occasionally in order to keep an eye on Alison, knowing that he had no way to communicate with her and that he had to keep her in sight lest they become separated. She and Maxine swam steadily ahead, moving side by side.

Nature was putting on a magnificent show for him. He thrilled to the unusual turmoil and activity, using his camera as an artist would a brush. So he was scarcely surprised when the view-finder picked up the protruding lips of a barracuda. This was what he had been after. What a brute! Its sleek, lean body looked like six feet of flashing steel, forged with deadly precision and tempered to a razor sharpness. No wonder the underwater world was in such a state of excitement—an excitement that Ralph now fully shared.

The barracuda swam diagonally above the two women, moving slowly, its cold eyes searching for hapless prey. A small fish, swimming barely three feet above Alison's shoulder, felt sudden death as fierce jaws clamped its body. The camera caught the maimed victim as it was flipped around and swallowed tail first.

In his excitement, Ralph moved nearer, hoping for a close-up of the slanting head, the vicious teeth protruding from the lower jaw. The barracuda was floating just above the women with an ominous placidity that was like the lull before the storm. As if by telepathy, Ralph realized the sinister intent just a split second before it happened—and by then it was too late.

With lightning swiftness, the monster shot like a giant arrow straight toward Alison. Ralph froze as his heart stopped beating. Time stood still in one long, awful eternity. As if in a ghastly nightmare, he was paralyzed, unable to move a muscle. Alison hadn't even seen the monster. She made a convulsive movement and the water around her grew turbid and then a red stain fanned out about her like the opening petals of a rose in a slow-motion movie.

The camera dropped from Ralph's hand and he raced toward her as fast as the fins would propel him. At the same time, Maxine clutched Alison's arm and held her tight.

The attacker moved a few yards away and lurked menacingly behind a ledge of coral, sizing them up for his next savage run. Ralph reached the women and grabbed Alison's free hand. Frantically he and Maxine swam with her to a small crevice in the reef. Through the mask her eyes were round with shock; her skin was deathly white.

Ralph grabbed at a jutting point of coral and held fast to the reef. The jagged edges cut through his canvas gloves. Desperately he thought that if they could stay out of sight, the barracuda might move on to other prey, but in his heart he knew that this could not be. The blood in the water would whet its insane appetite, luring it back again and again until its cold, evil greed was sated. And Ralph knew from the time gauge on Alison's tank that they could not stay submerged for long.

He and Maxine clung tenaciously to the ledge and waited, partners suddenly in the grimmest battle of all—the fight for survival. Ralph's free hand clamped like a vice over the gaping wound in the girl's shoulder but the throbbing flow of blood continued with each heartbeat and he saw that in a few minutes she would lose consciousness.

He knew that if she were to be saved, she must be taken to the surface. But this required crawling hundreds of feet along the coral wall with her for directly above them was a completely impenetrable ceiling of coral outcroppings and tunneled ledges. And leaving the crevice would bring certain attack—and, ultimately, certain death for all of them. Already the barracuda was moving closer, circling lazily in the water, getting set for the bloody kill.

There was only one possible way out. It was a long shot but what had they to lose? Anything would be better than clinging to the crevice, waiting. At least they didn't have to commit suicide, did they? One of them could carry Alison to safety while the other acted as a decoy. He shuddered in a huge spasm as his heart constricted painfully at the thought.

He glanced quickly at Maxine and the expression in her eyes told him that she was thinking the same thing. He realized that their situations were equal. Both of them were strong swimmers, either one could take Alison to safety, and they were both in love with her. Each wanted life only if it meant life with Alison . . . and each would make the final sacrifice in order to save her.

If we had a coin, he thought bitterly, we could flip it.

But the decision, they both strangely realized, rested with Alison. Thus far she had had them both on her own terms. Now she must choose between them. Finally and irrevocably. Ralph wondered if she weren't to be pitied the most of all.

She had been watching them, her eyes half closed with pain and fatigue, her body weak and helpless. He could not tell whether she was expecting them to solve the situation, whether she accepted their lot as final, even whether she understood the situation in all its details. With one hand he indicated to her that the time had come to move and that one of them would carry her. He prayed, for her sake, that she might never know the enormity of her decision. Yet he knew that, in the desperation and unselfconsciousness of her suffering, the choice she would make would be the honest one.

Holding fast to the ledge with one hand, Maxine moved in front of Alison and put out an arm to help her. Instantly Ralph was beside her. Alison looked into Ralph's eyes and then into Maxine's. She gazed at her for a long moment. Ralph saw a faint smile of relief cross Maxine's face. He stopped breathing. He should have known it all along. He closed his eyes, struggling for a breath of air. What difference did it make now, anyway? Just let him breathe long enough to do the job that had to be done.

Then, like a sleepy child, Alison turned to him and let her head rest on his shoulder. Momentarily stunned, he reacted automatically and put one arm diagonally across her back, grasping her firmly. Then he turned to look at Maxine, deep sorrow for her etched across his face. Behind the mask her features were contorted with an agony that had nothing to do with the prospect of death. She had just lost the only thing that made life worth living. Death, to her, would be sweet.

She bent to retrieve the light that Alison had dropped. Then, as if in a trance, she swam off slowly down the passage toward the lagoon. Max, Ralph's thoughts cried after her. Max! I'm sorry it turned out this way for you. So terribly sorry. You'll never know, Max, but I didn't really mean to hurt you, not this way. I'll be good to her, Max. I'll give her everything you could have given, and more. I'll give her everything, Max. I promise you.

The barracuda drew away, distracted from the scent of blood by the strange, shimmering thing moving through the water.

Dazedly Ralph began to push his way along the passage. He did not look back again for fear that he would go utterly mad. Alison hung limp in his arm, bobbing like a rag doll, her head rolling from side to side.

They moved down the coral corridor inch by inch like some huge, creeping crustacean. The coral had shredded his gloves, bitten into his hands, raked his back, but he felt no pain. He wanted to shout at her, *Breathe, darling, breathe. Keep the bubbles rising so I know you are all right.* But he could make no sound. He could only keep moving forward in silence and fear.

A trickle of light green filtered its way down through the blackness. He took a deep breath and with the last bit of his strength, pulled her close to him and shot for the surface. He swam with her free of the reef and held her head and the wounded shoulder clear of the water. He searched frantically for the sight of a boat.

Exactly where they had left it, the *Jim Boy* floated languidly at anchor. He could hear the sounds of the women's voices, laughing, still having a picnic, waiting for them to return. Thank God, he thought, Judy had not trusted him after all, even with Maxine along. He pulled the mask from his face and shouted hoarsely for help.

Would they ever hear?

He saw a faint stir of life. The dinghy went over the side, and then he caught the gleam of Noah's strong black arms pulling the craft toward them.

A few minutes later Ralph handed Alison aboard the skiff and pulled himself painfully after her. She lay against the thwart without moving. Ralph took off her mask and looked, terrified, into the small, still face.

They reached the yacht and Judy yelled down. "Don't move her!" Judy came rapidly down the rope ladder, a first-aid kit in her hand.

Together they loosened the rest of the bulky apparatus. Judy looked at the gash in the girl's flesh and moved hastily to quench the flow of blood. He kneeled in the boat beside her, watching the blood soak through the wad of cloth. Judy's fingers worked rapidly, skillfully.

She looked up at him only once. She said simply, "Max?"

He shrugged and lifted his hands helplessly.

She sighed, glancing at his torn flesh, his horror-stricken eyes. "I guess you tried," she murmured. She turned back to Alison.

He did not know how long he squatted there, watching, waiting, praying. But finally he saw Judy take Alison's wrist between her fingers and heard her expel a long breath. He looked at her silently, afraid to ask the question.

She nodded. "Just in time," she said. "We'll have to get her to the hospital fast, but she'll be okay."

He turned away from her then so that she would not see the tears in his eyes. He looked off toward the island and the reef and in his heart sent out a silent tribute to Maxine. Whatever she had done, whatever she had been, he could never hate her again—for she had given him the gift of life.

"Look!" Judy said behind him.

Alison had opened her eyes. She stared blindly in front of her, her face twitching with anguish, trying to remember. He went to her quickly and bent down beside her. He took her hand and raised it to his lips. "Darling," he said.

She blinked her eyes to bring him into focus. The worry, the anguish, faded and she smiled.

"Oh, my darling," she whispered.

THE END